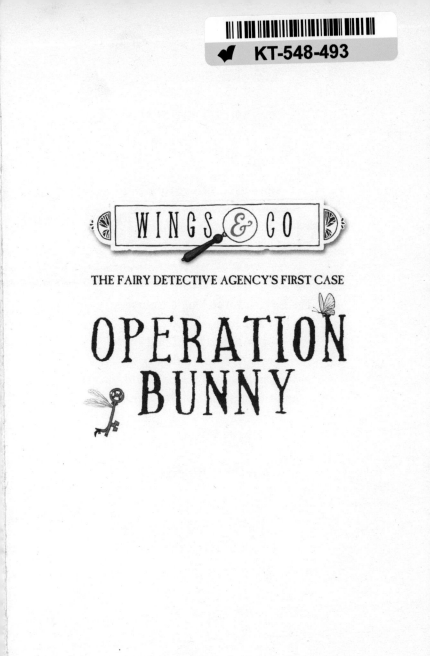

WINGS & CO

THE FAIRY DETECTIVE AGENCY'S FIRST CASE

OPERATION BUNNY

Also by Sally Gardner

Look out for the next

 WINGS & CO

detective adventure

Three Pickled Herrings

SALLY GARDNER

Illustrated by
David Roberts

WINGS & CO

THE FAIRY DETECTIVE AGENCY'S FIRST CASE

OPERATION
BUNNY

Orion
Children's Books

First published in Great Britain in 2012
by Orion Children's Books
a division of the Orion Publishing Group Ltd
Orion House
5 Upper St Martin's Lane
London WC2H 9EA
A Hachette UK Company

9 10 8

Text copyright © Sally Gardner 2012
Illustrations copyright © David Roberts 2012

A catalogue record for this book is available from the British Library.

ISBN 978 1 4440 0372 7

Printed and bound in Great Britain

The Orion Publishing Group's policy is to use papers that are natural,
renewable and recyclable products made from wood grown in sustainable
forests. The logging and manufacturing processes are expected to
conform to the environmental regulations of the country of origin.

www.orionbooks.co.uk

For Ellen Butler, my dearest friend.

With love, S

Chapter One

Daisy Dashwood and Ronald Dashwood had everything a young couple could dream of: a house in the suburbs, with box hedges shaped like squirrels, two cars in the drive with customised number plates – HER1 and HIS2, a tennis court, a small swimming pool, a gym. They even owned a villa near Malaga in Spain. But the one thing they didn't have, the one thing neither money nor nature had been able to give them, was a baby.

Their next door neighbour, Miss String, had suggested kindly that perhaps Daisy should make a wish.

'A wish,' said Daisy Dashwood. 'The cheek of the nosy old bat. As if you get anything by wishing.'

'Quite right, Smoochikins,' replied her husband. 'Best to believe in facts and figures, not in airy-fairy wishes and daft stuff like that.'

Ronald knew about such things. He had made his money as a hedge fund manager – whatever a hedge fund manager was. Daisy couldn't agree more. She trusted in her credit cards: silver, gold and platinum.

Miss String's house was a real eyesore. At least, that's what Daisy called it.

It had crooked turrets and large windows and a charm that the Dashwoods' house would never possess in a thousand years. Miss String's ancestors had once owned all the surrounding countryside. Bit by bit, the huge estate had been nibbled away by debt until finally Miss String had been forced to sell the remaining land, leaving her with only the house and garden.

Now Miss String's house sat in the middle of three bossy buildings, every one of her wealthy neighbours wanting a slice more of her large garden for themselves.

It was Ronald Dashwood who had made what he considered to be a wildly generous offer for nearly all of the garden. This would have left Miss String a small patio at the back and a footpath at the front so that she could get into her house.

'The cheek of the old bat,' said Daisy Dashwood when Ronald's offer was turned down. 'What does she need so much garden for? And the vegetable plot? Oh, my days, hasn't the woman heard of home deliveries? The next thing she'll be telling us is that she doesn't own a computer, or even a TV.'

On both counts Daisy Dashwood was correct. The modern world had somehow passed by Miss String and Fidget, her cat. The closest it had ever come to knocking on her front door was the dreadful collection of 'executive' homes that had sprung up around her. Whatever 'executive' meant.

One summer's morning, the Dashwoods were eating breakfast when Daisy spotted a headline in the newspaper.

BABY THOUGHT TO BE A BOMB.

'Listen to this, Ronald.'

'What, Smoochikins?'

9

'It says, "Yesterday Stansted Airport was closed from ten o'clock in the morning until four in the afternoon, causing –"' Daisy paused, '"pan-de-mon-ium. A hatbox believed to contain an explosive device had been left in the main concourse of the terminal. Andrew Vole, 46, head of the bomb disposal team, said ticking could be heard coming from inside.

'It was a very good thing,' he added, 'that the baby started crying before we did our controlled explosion.'

When the lid was removed, a baby girl, less than three months old, was found lying in blue tissue paper. Beside her was a trick clock with a cuckoo that squirted water.

The police are now searching for the owner of the hatbox, who they suspect to be the mother of the infant. They said they had nothing to go on other than the name printed on the hatbox – Emily's Millinery.

For the time being the baby is being cared

for at Cherryfield Orphanage. A nurse has named her Emily after the hatbox and Vole after the bomb disposal officer." '

Daisy paused, then said 'Ronald', in a voice that sounded like a cross between a whine and a peacock scream. It was the special voice she used when she wanted something expensive or difficult to get.

'I am all ears,' said Ronald, and he was. He had a shocking pair of red, sticking-out ears. In fact, they were the first thing you noticed about him.

'What I wish . . .' said Daisy.

'What I know,' interrupted Ronald, 'is that you *never* wish, Smoochikins.'

'Well, I'm going to make an exception, just this once.'

'All right,' said Ronald. 'What is it you wish for?'

'I wish that baby was mine.'

Ronald smiled lovingly at his credit card-munching wife and said, 'Whatever little Smoochikins wants, she shall have.'

And in less time than it took to grow mint, the Dashwoods had adopted Emily Vole.

As Fidget the cat said to Miss String on hearing the news, a wish can be a dangerous thing.

'I agree,' sighed Miss String as they sat in their enchanting garden one afternoon while the kettle was busy making the tea. 'Perhaps I shouldn't have said anything.'

'Always best,' agreed Fidget. 'Humans, in my considered opinion, don't think things through, especially when it comes to wishes.'

Which was quite right. Daisy Dashwood never thought at all if she could help it. She had just made a wish. Why, isn't that what everyone does? Make a wish – it's easy-peasy.

Chapter Two

Five years later, Daisy Dashwood had to admit that Emily Vole wasn't exactly what she had had in mind when she'd made her one and only wish. What she had really wanted was a baby girl with blue eyes and blonde hair, ideally the same colour as her own strawberry-blonde hair extensions.

The trouble was that Emily's eyes were far too dark for her to be a true Dashwood offspring. But worse than the ebony eyes was Emily's hair. It was jet black.

Not even Daisy, the proud owner of Paradise Beauty Salon, could do anything to improve the situation. There was no getting away from it. The child just didn't fit in with the Dashwoods' ancestral colour scheme.

Fortunately, Emily was brighter than a pearly queen's button, brighter by far than her two adoptive parents. At three, she was well aware she was not what Daisy had wished for. By four, she had grown used to wearing the blonde wig and the blue contact lenses. By five, she had an inkling of what was to come the minute she heard that Daisy Dashwood was pregnant.

'Oh, my days. Triplets,' said Daisy. 'Well, now we definitely don't need Emily. Could we send her back to the orphanage? I have the receipt for her somewhere.'

'Not really, Smoochikins,' replied Ronald, watching his wife rummage in her real alligator handbag. 'It wasn't a receipt, it was the adoption papers.'

'Well then, we can say she was a dress rehearsal and we don't need her any more, seeing as we have three coming our way.'

'It wouldn't sound good, Smoochikins.'

'I can't cope,' said Daisy, raising her hands in the air. 'It's all too much. I tell you, it's all too much.'

'There is always boarding school,' suggested Ronald helpfully. 'Then we need only see the brat in the holidays.'

Daisy Dashwood's hopes of being rid of Emily were somewhat blighted in that department too. Wrenworth School only took boarders from the age of nine. Everywhere that did take younger girls cost at least thirteen designer handbags a term.

"I have an idea,' said Ronald to his ever-expanding wife. 'Perhaps it is the best idea I've come up with in ages.'

'Go on then, don't keep me in suspenders, spit it out.'

'We make Emily earn her keep.'

'How?' asked Daisy.

'With three little pairs of feet on the way we will need all the help we can get and—'

'That's genius,' interrupted Daisy. 'We'll tell any nosy busybody who asks about Emily that she is being home educated. Which is the truth. We are educating her to be a nanny and a housekeeper.'

That was when Emily Vole found out she had lost her job as the Dashwoods' adopted daughter. The blonde wig and the blue contact lenses vanished. So did the pink bedroom, which wasn't all bad. Pink was a colour

Emily hated. It did come as a surprise to find that she was expected to sleep in the laundry room alongside

the washing machine and the tumble dryer. Her bed was to be the ironing board.

Never once did it cross the Dashwoods' minds that Emily was far too young to be left in charge. All they cared about was that the house was kept neat and tidy.

Daisy had no intention of staying at home. Every day she went off to work.

'But, Smoochikins,' said Ronald. 'You should be resting, not working at your beauty salon. After all, you have three little pairs of hands inside you. And three little pairs of feet. That makes thirty little fingers and thirty little toe nails. Not to mention three brains.'

'Oh, shut up. That's disgusting,' said Daisy. 'Of course I'm going to work. Who, other than me, will check on my staff? I have a lot of people's hair extensions resting in my hands. They rely on me. There's no way I'm staying in the house all day becoming fatter than a fairground balloon. Emily will run the house.'

And run the house Emily did.

Chapter Three

The role of general dogsbody turned out to be a lot harder than the role of adopted daughter with wig. At least as adopted daughter Emily had been able to wear pretty dresses and had a bedroom full of toys. Although there were no books, which was a pity because Emily loved stories.

When Emily heard that the Dashwoods were expecting triplets, she had hoped that she might be returned to the orphanage. There was no doubt in her mind that her real parents were looking for her. It had been a bitter blow to find she was to go no farther than the laundry room.

Emily had decided that really she was the daughter of a princess who had fallen in love with a gypsy. He had won the young princess's heart by baking cupcakes with red and green icing, her favourite colours. The lovers ran away to the magic forest where they were married by fairies.

One terrible day the princess's father, the king, discovered his daughter's hiding place. He ordered the magic forest to be chopped down unless she returned to the palace. The fairies told Emily's parents they would be very much missed but begged them to be gone. Before the king could do his worst, the gypsy and the princess hurriedly put their baby daughter into a hatbox. With the help of a fairy charm – the trick clock – the baby slept peacefully. Outside the hatbox, the terrifying chase was on. Her parents, quite out of breath, finally arrived at Stansted Airport. The king's soldiers were waiting to snatch the princess.  The gypsy put up a noble fight as they ran for the departure gate. But he was wounded in the arm, and the hatbox slipped from his grasp as they made their escape. The king's soldiers didn't know there was a baby inside and returned, empty-handed, to face the fury of the king.

It was, thought Emily, a very sad story indeed.

She was determined that one day she would run away and find her parents. She had begun to collect things she might need. So far she had one packet of biscuits and a little cardboard suitcase with a lock on it that she'd found in the recycling bin.

It was a letter from Social Services that finally forced the Dashwoods to buy Emily her one and only book. The social worker, Ms Rogers, was worried that Emily Vole-Dashwood hadn't been enrolled at any of the local schools. She was extremely anxious to know why.

'The blooming cheek of the nosy old batskin,' said Daisy. 'What do we do, Ronald?'

'Buy her a book?' said Ronald. 'The kind of thing you need to show we are home educating her.'

'Couldn't we just show her doing the ironing?' said Daisy. 'I mean, that's an important lesson.'

'I don't think it would wash,' replied Ronald.

A week later, Emily was given a book of fairy tales.

Every night, she sat on her ironing-board bed, holding the garden torch and staring open-mouthed at all the pictures. She couldn't read the words but there was enough to look at for Emily's imagination to fill in the gaps.

The world began to make more sense. Emily imagined herself to be in need of a gentle lady with wings and a pumpkin to help her escape, though one glass slipper wouldn't do it. It would have to be two, otherwise she would never get away. The picture Emily liked best was of the big cat in a pair of boots that nearly drowned him. Whatever it was he said to the king when he stopped his carriage, everything turned out sunshine-dandy.

'Mrs Dashwood,' said Emily seriously. She no longer addressed her as Adoptive Mother.

'What?' said Daisy, spread-eagled on the sofa. Her tummy appeared to have a life of its own. It moved in a wriggly-piggly fashion.

'May I ask you a question?' said Emily.

'Yes,' said Mrs Dashwood. 'But make it quick.'

'Do cats talk?' asked Emily.

'What kind of daft question is that? Don't you know anything?'

'It's just a question,' said Emily.

'Oh, my days. We have the stupidest housekeeper ever. Of course they don't talk, just as cows don't go over the moon. What is in that brain of yours? Sawdust?'

The social worker came round only once to enquire after Emily and why she was not at school. By then, Daisy looked fit to burst with all those fingers and toes.

'We are home educating the little sunflower,' she said to the social worker in a voice of which a screeching parrot would have been proud. 'You see, Emily is not very bright. I am afraid she has special needs.'

'What special needs?' asked the social worker.

'Oh, you know, the kind that come from being abandoned in a hatbox.'

The social worker, seeing the showroom wife in the glimmering show house, thought Emily was a very lucky little girl to live in such a fine home.

Sadly, this is often the way. Through the windows of poorer houses the need for help is easier to see. Money can hide almost anything and the Dashwoods had enough to hide Emily completely from view.

Chapter Four

When the triplets were born they were named Peach, Petal and Plum. All had sticking-out red ears like their father's, all had blue eyes and strawberry-blonde hair just like their mother's. The Dashwoods were the proudest parents ever. Every oochy-coochy-poo, every twinkle-winkle was recorded on camera. Every gurgly smile greeted with joy. There was no doubt in the Dashwoods' minds that they had produced the cleverest three babies in the world. In short, they were besotted in a way they had never been with Emily.

The camera had never recorded Emily's first smile, steps or words. Daisy had been bored stiff by Emily as a baby and hadn't become any more interested as Emily grew older. As far as Daisy was concerned Emily had been a tiresome, talkative toddler.

'How can a child be so stuffed full of *why*s?' Daisy had moaned to Ronald.

'I don't know, Smoochikins.'

Now, to the Dashwoods, Emily was as good as invisible.

In the first year of the triplets' lives, Emily spent nearly all her time rushing round filling babies' bottles, changing nappies, loading and unloading the washing machine, and generally working her socks off.

After the triplets' second birthday, Emily found that at least she had a break in the days when Daisy put them in the car and went to spend the afternoon being Queen Bee at the local mothers' meeting.

On Very Wonderful Days, as Emily called them, Daisy and the triplets would leave in the morning and return home at five o'clock, having enjoyed the benefits of Macreedy's Health, Wealth and Beauty Club where there was a crèche.

On one of these Very Wonderful Days, when the house was blissfully quiet, Emily decided she would hang the sheets and the nappies outside on the washing line. She thought they would smell sweeter if they dried in the fresh air. Emily found a ladder tucked away in the garage. It was wooden and wobbly and it was quite a juggling act on Emily's part to carry it into the garden. With pegs in one hand and washing in the other she climbed to the top of the wobbly, wooden ladder. She had rather hoped that once up there she might at long last get a chance to see over the Dashwoods' neat squirrel box hedges into the neighbour's garden. But pegging all those wet clothes to the washing line while keeping her balance was far harder than she had imagined.

Emily had always thought she would like to meet Miss String. Especially as she knew that Ex-Adoptive Mother-stroke-Employer couldn't stand the old bat. That in itself was enough to make Emily sure that Miss String couldn't be at all bad.

By teatime the laundry looked dry. Emily once more climbed the wobbly, wooden ladder. This time, before tackling the troublesome matter of unpegging the washing, she was determined to see properly into Miss

String's garden. It was full of flowers. There was even a vegetable patch with a scarecrow stuck in the middle. The house beamed a sunshine smile through its windows. Emily thought it looked not unlike a picture from her fairy tale book. She was so taken with the view that she forgot to be careful on top of the wobbly, wooden ladder and lost her balance. Sheets, nappies and Emily all crashed to the ground.

Emily knew there was no point in bursting into tears. No one would come. Anyway, she was pretty certain that nothing was broken. She was studying her wounds – a grazed knee and a sore elbow – when she heard a rustling sound from the squirrel box hedge. She looked up to see an enormous, long-haired, tortoiseshell cat, covered in leaves, pushing his way through the hedge. And this was the strange part: the cat wasn't on all fours like an ordinary cat. It was standing up.

Emily wondered if she might have banged her head on the way down because she was sure she heard the cat say, in a low, gruff voice, 'Are you all right, miss?'

A talking cat. Just like the fairy tale. It was good to know that her ex-adoptive mother wasn't right on all matters.

'Not really,' Emily said. 'I have—'

'Oh, my dear whiskers,' interrupted the cat. 'Stay put and don't do anything hasty.'

A talking cat, Emily thought, as he disappeared back through the hedge, is enough to take one's mind off all sorts of pains.

Chapter Five

Emily was still trying to work out whether or not she had imagined the talking cat when an elderly woman appeared beside her.

'Oh dear, oh dear, what a to-do,' she said rushing up to Emily and helping her to her feet. 'Fidget came to tell me that you had taken a nasty tumble. Anything broken?'

'No, I don't think so,' said Emily, 'but thank you very much for asking.'

'Capital,' said the lady. She had a round, rosy face with white hair that refused to stay pinned up to the top of her head. She looked a little like the fairy godmother in Emily's story book. Emily was sure this was Miss String.

'I expect you know me as "the old bat",' said the lady. Emily looked a bit sheepish. 'Mrs Dashwood is not related to me,' she said feebly.

Miss String laughed. 'I know that. And a jolly good thing too, if you don't mind me saying.'

By now, Fidget was back again, this time with a builder's apron tied round him.

Seeing the puzzled look on Emily's face, he said, 'Stops fur getting on things.'

Emily pinched herself. Fidget was now helping Miss String to fold the washing and put it neatly into the basket. As if neatly folding washing was something they did between them every day.

'Where do you want me to put this?' asked Fidget in a matter-of-fact way. He was extraordinarily strong for a cat. He picked up the basket with no trouble at all and took it into the kitchen.

'A tower of strength, is my Fidget,' said Miss String. 'Oh, Fidget,' she called after him. 'Don't forget to put away the ladder too. Where does it go, dear?' she asked Emily.

'The garage,' Emily managed to mutter.

'Capital,' replied Miss String. 'Now, come along, I have made fairy cakes with red and green sugar icing.'

Emily was even more flabbergasted. 'How did you know that those are my favourite colours?'

'Just a hunch that Fidget had. His hunches are, more often than not, spot on the trot. Call it animal instinct.'

Emily followed Miss String into her garden and sat in a chair. She let out a sigh.

Miss String asked, 'Does anything hurt?'

'Oh, no,' said Emily. 'It's just all perfect.'

'An overrated word,' said Fidget. 'Especially with cats of the feminine kind. They are always saying I'm purrrrrfect.'

'Fidget,' interrupted Miss String. 'Manners, please. We have a guest and that sort of talk isn't polite.'

'Sorry,' said Fidget. 'No damage done to the little ducks?'

'None,' said Emily. 'If I am the little ducks.'

'It's a pet name I've made up especially for you.'

'I've never had one of those,' said Emily.

This magical garden seemed to have little, if anything, to do with the modern world of the Dashwoods. Miss String wore a skirt which ballooned out at the bottom and ankle boots that turned up at the toes.

Fidget brought out a tea tray with the fairy cakes on it, then sat down in a deckchair next to his mistress looking very pleased with himself. The fairy cakes were delicious. The red icing tasted of strawberries and cream. The green icing tasted of apple pies.

'Fidget did the icing,' explained Miss String.

Emily ate three fairy cakes. This was the best afternoon she could ever remember. Suddenly she heard the sound of the four-wheel-drive on the gravel next door. Daisy and the triplets were home.

'I have to go,' said Emily, leaping up, brushing the crumbs from her apron and wiping her mouth.

'Take it easy, my little ducks,' said Fidget. 'Remember, you've just had a nasty fall.'

'You look spick and span,' said Miss String, leaning forward and taking Emily's hand. 'If you wouldn't mind,

36

be a dear and don't say a word about Fidget, and you-know-what.'

'The talking?' said Emily.

'Spot on the fishcake, my little ducks,' said Fidget.

'Not a word,' said Emily. 'I promise. Anyway, Mrs Dashwood wouldn't believe me. She doesn't believe in talking cats, or fairies, for that matter.'

At that, both Miss String and Fidget burst out laughing.

'More fool her,' said Fidget. 'That's all I can say.'

Emily was home just in time to be ready and waiting at the front door.

'You look as if you've been dragged through a hedge backwards,' said Daisy with Peach on one hip and Plum on the other.

'Sorry, Mrs Dashwood,' said Emily.

'Well, don't just stand there,' shouted Daisy. 'Go and get Petal out of her car seat and the shopping from the boot, then put the kettle on and get their tea ready and . . .'

Emily had stopped listening. For the first time ever she felt happy, certain there was a sunnier life waiting for her over the squirrel box hedge.

Chapter Six

By the time the triplets were two and a half, Daisy Dashwood had found them a theatrical agent.

'Talent like theirs,' Daisy told Ronald, 'mustn't be wasted.'

At three years old, Peach, Petal and Plum were earning good money as little models in TV adverts.

Meanwhile, Emily was left to slowly drown in piles of housework. Her ex-adoptive-mother-stroke-employer would set Emily little tests, leaving a small piece of paper under a lamp stand or a kettle, just to make sure Emily had cleaned all the surfaces properly. If Daisy found any of the pieces of paper in the evening, Emily was sent to bed without supper.

Emily's work was never up to scratch.

'I mean,' Daisy complained to Ronald, 'I leave her lists of things to do and they're never done.'

'Can she read, Smoochikins?' asked Ronald.

'How should I know?' said Daisy. 'She should be able to by now. She's eight years old.'

'Have you taught her?'

'Don't be daft, Ronald. When would I have time for that?'

Three days after Emily first met Miss String and her talking cat, they came to her rescue. Emily had so much wanted to see them again but she had never found time to slip through the hedge. They turned up one morning shortly after Daisy and the triplets had left for a day's filming.

'Frazzle my whiskers,' said Fidget, as he stared at the kitchen sink piled ceiling-high with dirty pots and pans.

The kitchen table looked as if a bomb had fallen. It was covered in broken egg shells, toasty fingers, butter, jam and cereal.

'It was the triplets' breakfast,' said Emily. 'I'm about to clean it up.'

'What else needs doing, dear?' asked Miss String kindly.

Emily showed her Daisy's unreadable list. Miss String read it out loud.

'Clean kitchen.

'Scrub pans.

'Sort out fridge.

'Scrub floor.

'Dust the lounge and the study.'

'Oh,' said Emily. 'That's what it says. I couldn't make head or tail of it.'

'She has the most dreadful writing,' said Miss String.

'The trouble is, I can't read or write,' said Emily. 'I'm trying to teach myself but it isn't really working. That's the morning list. And this is the afternoon one.'

'Ironing,' read Miss String. 'How much ironing?'

Emily opened the door to the laundry room, and showed them three huge baskets, each filled with a small mountain of crinkled clothes.

'Are you supposed to do all this by the end of the day?' said Miss String.

42

'Yes.'

'Buddleia, buddleia and buddleia again,' said Miss String.

'What does that mean?' asked Emily.

'It doesn't mean anything other than a bush that butterflies like, but the word has a good ring to it when one is cross,' said Miss String. 'And cross I am. How dare Mrs Dashwood make you her slave. Come on, Fidget. All paws and hands on deck.'

Miss String and Fidget whirled round the rooms so fast that Emily felt quite giddy. In less time than she thought possible, the house was spick and span.

'Thank you,' said Emily, when the whirling had come to a stop and the house sparkled and gleamed. 'Oh, thank you so much. This afternoon I can do the ironing.'

'Buddleia to all that,' said Miss String. 'Buddleia and bindweed.'

'Ironing while listening to cricket on the radio,' said Fidget, 'happens to be my favourite pastime. Apart from, that is, a good kipper and a good kip. One being a fish and the other a sleep. Now, why don't you two pad off and leave it to me. I am the cat's whisker of the ironing board.'

'Capital idea, Fidget. Come along, Emily,' Miss String said, taking Emily's hand. 'I am going to teach you to read and write.'

'You mean lessons?' said Emily, stunned. She turned back to see that Fidget had already started to sort the clothes. 'Can you read, Fidget?'

'I could, once,' he said, only half-listening. 'I lost interest when I was turned into a moggy. Well, you would, wouldn't you?'

'You were human? Who turned you into a cat?'

'Now, now,' said Miss String. 'Enough of that, Fidget.'

That day was the start of Emily's education. In the morning she would wait for Daisy and the triplets to leave, then wait a little bit longer just in case Daisy had forgotten anything, which she nearly always had. Once the coast was clear, Fidget and Miss String would pop round to lick the house into shape. In no time at all the three of them had worked out a routine that meant Emily had nearly all day for her lessons. It was the first time in Emily's life that she could remember being happy. Happy, she thought, as in ever after.

Daisy Dashwood no longer had any complaints about Emily's housekeeping.

'All this home education is paying off,' said Daisy, and sneezed. 'I told you she would teach herself.' She sneezed again.

'Smoochikins,' said Ronald. 'Are you all right?'

Daisy sneezed a third time.

'You only sneeze,' said Ronald, 'when you are around cats.'

'We don't have a cat,' said Daisy, sneezing again and again.

Chapter Seven

Within a year Emily could read, write, do maths and speak fluent French and German. Plus another strange language that Miss String called Old English.

'It may not be needed,' she said, 'but you never know, these days.'

Of the many stories Miss String told Emily, the ones she liked best of all had to do with a very strange shop.

'Back in the days long ago,' said Miss String, 'there was a shop run by the fairy folk.'

'What was it called?' Emily asked.

'Wings & Co,' replied Miss String. 'It sold potions and lotions but that was more by the by. Most people who visited the shop came because they needed the help of the fairies.'

'What sort of help?' said Emily, feeling a tingle of excitement.

'In solving riddles,' said Miss String. 'Finding things that were lost. Untangling a mystery or two.'

'That's just the kind of thing I would like to do,' said Emily. 'What sort of mysteries were they?'

But Miss String would say nothing more about the fairies. But she did tell Emily about the shop.

'It was built on four long, iron legs that bent at the knees; each leg had three griffin's talons at the bottom with steel claws . . .'

'Why did it have legs?' Emily asked.

'Simple,' said Miss String. 'So it could walk from town to town. When it came to a place it liked, its dragon feet would dig deep into the earth so that the shop wouldn't blow away in the wind and rain.'

Emily wondered if there were other buildings that could do the same thing or if this shop was the only one in the world. She never managed to ask the question, for there was so much more to the shop than its legs.

'The shop had another secret,' said Miss String.

'Oh – what?' asked Emily.

'The upstairs rooms could twist and turn themselves around and inside out. Very handy if, for instance, an unwanted highwayman came calling, for no matter how many doors he might open and close trying to get out, he wouldn't be able to unless the shop let him go.'

'Wow, that is real magic,' said Emily. 'Who built the shop?'

'It was designed by one of the most famous magicians of his day and built by the Queen's own master builder.'

At the time Miss String first told Emily the story of the shop, they were studying the glorious Queen Elizabeth I, who, according to Miss String, was the first and last 'Faerie Queene' of England.

Miss String had a treasure to go with every period they studied, from the Vikings onwards. Now they had reached the Tudors. All the treasures from those days were hidden in the attic, in a heavy, painted oak chest. Fidget had to bring it down. He was none too pleased.

'Do you think this is wise?' he asked Miss String. 'It's making my fur itch already.'

'Perhaps you need the flea treatment again?'

If a cat could look cross, Fidget managed it.

'There is not one flea on me. Personally, I would kipper this period of history, and you know why.'

'Why?' asked Emily.

'Because that's when I was turned into a cat.'

'Enough,' said Miss String.

'Still,' mumbled Fidget. 'I think it's best to let sleeping keys lie.' Seeing that Miss String wasn't listening, Fidget said, 'Tea?'

'Oh, yes please,' said Emily.

'*Faerie* cakes?' he said very pointedly to Miss String, as if he meant something else altogether.

'Capital,' replied Miss String, opening the heavy lid of the chest. 'Just the ticket.'

Inside, wrapped carefully in tissue paper, was a lace ruff. It had been worn, so Miss String said, by an ancient ancestor of hers. There was also a pair of dainty embroidered gloves. Whoever owned them had had very small hands indeed. But what caught Emily's attention more than the lace ruff or the flattened suede gloves was a tiny bunch of golden keys, each key elaborately carved. There were seventeen in all, held together on a large, golden ring.

'Best not to touch them, dear,' said Miss String. 'They can give one a nasty scratch if they have a mind to.'

Too late. Emily had already picked up the keys. Then something wondrous happened.

To her amazement, the tiny keys each sprouted one leg and on the end of each leg was a laced-up boot. The keys all stood up together, rather gingerly at first. Emily was half-expecting to hear them talk for they seemed very excited, jumping up and down, falling over again and scrabbling to their feet, only to repeat the whole exercise. Emily soon realised the reason for this was that their boot laces were all knotted together.

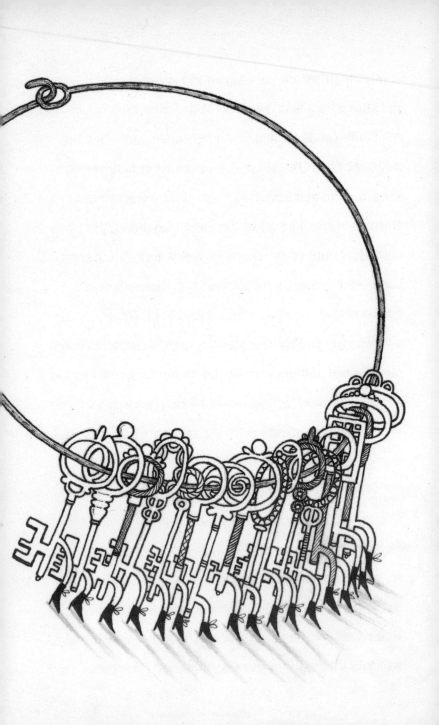

Gently she lifted the tiny bunch of keys on to a table.

Miss String hadn't said a word.

Emily sat down and patiently untied and retied the tiny boot laces. The keys were delighted at being freed and stood up and bowed to Emily. Emily was thrilled. This was real magic, just like in her fairy book.

Fidget entered the room, whereupon the keys, still bunched together on the golden ring, made a mad dash for the end of the table. Emily saved them from coming a cropper by putting them down on the floor. Here they ran, skipped and hopped around the room before coming back to her, bowing, then dashing merrily away again.

'Blow my whiskers off!' said Fidget, nearly dropping the tea tray.

'Are they a toy?' asked Emily.

'Oh no, dear,' said Miss String.

'What are they, then?'

'Keys,' said Fidget.

'That's right,' said Miss String, her voice a bit on the shaky side. 'They belonged to the magician who designed the shop I told you about. He put a spell on them so only he could use them, but I'm sorry to say he was killed by a witch. Since then, no fairy, elf or goblin has been able to break the spell and become Keeper of the Keys. You . . . er . . . you seem to have done the trick.'

That afternoon, as Miss String and Fidget watched Emily make her way back through the hedge to the Dashwoods' house, Fidget said, 'I had a feeling all along that she was special.'

'Yes,' said Miss String. 'So did I. Do you think Harpella heard the keys running about?'

'I hope not. But she has ears that can hear a butterfly fart,' said Fidget. He went down on all fours. The keys were shining shyly under the desk. Standing up, Fidget said, 'I have the advantage of nine lives, eight of which are still available to me. You, old girl, on the other paw, have only one. You need to take action, otherwise . . . well, the otherwise is a fur ball in my throat.'

'You are right,' said Miss String. She picked up the phone.

'Who are you calling?' asked Fidget.

'Alfred Twizell. He will know what needs to be done.'

'Alfred. Ottoline String here,' said Miss String. 'The you-know-what seem to have found a new keeper.'

There was silence on the line, then, 'A new keeper, you say?' said Alfred Twizell. Miss String could tell by the tone of his voice that he was excited. 'Who? Who is it?'

'A little girl called Emily Vole.'

'When did this happen?'

'Today. We opened the chest where your Elizabethan ruff and gloves are kept along with the keys. I didn't think for a moment  that anything would happen. Oh, Alfred, it is a gold letter day if ever there was one. We've waited half a millennium for this!'

Alfred replied almost in a whisper. 'You'd better come and see me straight away. Emily Vole will need protection.'

'I hadn't thought of that.'

'And, my dear Miss String,' said Alfred Twizell, 'please take care.'

Chapter Eight

Mr Charlie Cuddle, 98, was driving along Broad Street when he saw a witch on a broomstick. She appeared to be heading straight for him. That's when Mr Cuddle's foot slipped off the brake on to the accelerator, and he ran over Miss Ottoline String.

Emily knew nothing of this until much later that day. She wasn't worried that neither Fidget nor Miss String had come round to help. How could they when Daisy and the triplets were stuck at home? The children had been cast to appear as three peas in an advertising campaign for frozen vegetables and had been filming yesterday. Now their skin was stained green, their blonde hair the colour of mould. Daisy blamed the make-up department and demanded that someone come and sort this mess out right away, otherwise she would sue.

Just after lunch the doorbell rang. Daisy grabbed hold of Emily.

'Now, not a squeak from you – or else,' she said, locking Emily in the laundry room.

Daisy opened the front door. Standing there was a very tall woman. She wore neon orange platform shoes and had to stoop to get into the hall. Her hair was bright pink with purple streaks, she had a very fine nose, red lips, and enormous eyes that swam around like piranhas in a pond. She was dressed from head to toe in designer clothes.

Stooping towards Daisy, she held out a long, thin hand with steel-red fingernails.

'I am Doris Harper,' she said, but withdrew her hand as if scalded when Daisy tried to shake it. Doris Harper sniffed. Then sniffed again.

'Are you from the make-up department?' asked Daisy.

'I might as well be,' replied the woman.

'Oh, thank goodness,' said Daisy.

At that moment, the three cutiekins rushed from the kitchen on yet another round of demolition. They banged

into Ms Harper and, without a 'sorry' between them, rushed up the stairs sounding like a small herd of hippos.

Emily had no way of seeing all this, locked as she was in the laundry room. Still, she didn't like the sound of Doris Harper's icy voice one bit. She heard the triplets rush back into the kitchen, screaming, and then all was eerily quiet.

'My word,' Daisy Dashwood said. 'You do have a knack with children.'

'You have another child?' said Doris Harper.

'No,' said Daisy.

'Liar, liar, pants on fire,' said Ms Harper coldly.

'My daughters' skin,' said Daisy. 'It's tinged green.'

Emily could tell from Daisy's voice that she was worried. What the triplets were doing, Emily couldn't think, for they were never this quiet. 'Tomorrow,' said Daisy in a high-pitched squeal, 'they have an audition to be the Fairy Godmother's little fairy helpers in the Chrimbo panto.'

There was silence and Emily thought they must all have gone to the upstairs bathroom. She nearly jumped out of her skin when she saw an eye peering through the slatted blinds of the window. She hid as best she could, her heart beating double-fast.

'Cooeee, Ms Harper,' called Daisy. 'You forgot this.'

And the eye disappeared.

Emily's ear was now firmly glued to the laundry room door.

'It's a very unusual broom,' said Daisy. 'Is it a prop for a children's play?'

Emily couldn't catch the reply. The front door closed.

Ronald Dashwood returned home that evening to find his three daughters sitting as still as dolls in front of the television. He gave each one a kiss.

'Do you notice anything different about them?' Daisy asked him.

'Yes, I notice that for once our cutiekins are quiet, like good girls should be.'

'They just don't seem themselves,' said Daisy. 'Ever since that woman from the make-up department came.'

'She seems to have done the job,' said Ronald.
'No green skin. Smoochikins, don't look so worried.
Everything is fine, isn't it, girls?'

'Yes, Father,' they replied together. 'Everything's just
fine.'

'Quite,' said Ronald, a little less sure.

He took off his jacket, poured himself a stiff drink
and pulled out the evening paper.

'Listen to this, Smoochikins,' he said. 'You heard
about the car smash in Broad Street, didn't you?'

Daisy's mind was elsewhere but Emily was listening
as she loaded the dishwasher.

'It's been on the local radio all day,' continued
Ronald. 'You'll like this. "Mr Charlie Cuddle, 98,
said the reason he lost control of the car was
because he saw a witch on a broomstick. She
had flaming pink and purple hair and bright
orange shoes."' Ronald stopped. 'This is the best bit,
listen. "Mrs Cuddle, 86, of Pond Street, said her
husband was always seeing things and last
week saw a unicorn in the garden."' Ronald burst

out laughing. 'I know, it's not funny, but it is. "The police suspect the real reason for the accident was that Mr Cuddle was driving in his bedroom slippers."'

For a reason Emily didn't understand she felt a cold shiver go down her spine.

The doorbell rang. Daisy went to answer it.

'There must be some mistake,' Emily heard Daisy say to a softly spoken woman. 'Someone from the make-up department has already been.'

Then Emily knew for certain that something terrible had happened.

'Was anyone hurt in the accident?' she asked Ronald.

'Yes,' said Ronald. 'It's a bit of luck for us. It was the old bat next door.'

Chapter Nine

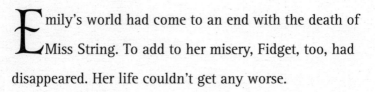

Emily's world had come to an end with the death of Miss String. To add to her misery, Fidget, too, had disappeared. Her life couldn't get any worse.

She decided two things. Firstly, she would not be the Dashwoods' adopted slave any more. Secondly, she would finally put her plan into action and run away.

Daisy Dashwood was beside herself with worry. Not about Emily, of course. No, it was her three cutiekins. Ever since Doris Harper's visit, Peach, Petal and Plum had become zombies.

The doctor examined them. He told Mrs Dashwood that they were all perfectly healthy – and beautifully behaved.

'That's the trouble,' wailed Daisy Dashwood. 'They're not themselves! Before, they could wreck a house if they put their minds to it.'

'Isn't this better?' said the doctor kindly.

'You don't understand,' wept Daisy. 'Someone has stolen my girls.'

'Mrs Dashwood,' said the doctor. 'You seem to be under a lot of stress.'

'I'm fine,' said Daisy, 'but my girls are gone.'

'No, Mrs Dashwood,' said the doctor. 'They are next door watching TV.' The tone of his voice had changed now. He was certain Mrs Dashwood was quite bonkers.

Daisy let Emily out of the laundry room when the doctor had left.

'The dishwasher needs emptying, the toilets need scrubbing, and so do the baths. Then you can hoover the house from top to bottom.'

Emily took a deep breath. 'No,' she said.

'No?' repeated Daisy.

'No,' said Emily. 'I won't, and I don't care what you do about it.'

Daisy's mouth fell open. Never in all her life had Emily spoken to Daisy like this.

'Oh, my days. As if I don't have enough to worry about! You will do as you are told and that's the end of it.' She stopped. 'I have a headache. I'm going to lie down. When I come back down I want everything to be spick and span. And no more smart talk.'

Emily went to find Peach, Petal and Plum. They were in the lounge, sitting log-still on the sofa, staring vacantly at the television.

'Peach,' said Emily. 'You are to unload the dishwasher. Plum, you are to clean the loos and the baths. Petal, you are to hoover the whole house from top to bottom.'

The three zombies went to work. For the first time in ages Emily sat down and watched a television programme. It was a detective series in which an old lady, who knitted, seemed able to solve all sorts of crimes. Emily thought that's what she wanted to be, not old or knitting, but a detective. And then she would solve the mystery of her missing parents.

These thoughts were interrupted when Daisy Dashwood woke up, saw what was happening, charged into the lounge and unplugged the TV.

'How dare you make my little cutiekins do all the work for you,' she said. 'When Ronald comes home he will deal with you, miss.'

As Emily didn't care any more about anything, she said, 'I am nine years old. Since the age of five I have worked for you day and night. I have never been given a birthday present, a Chrimbo present, as you call it, or even an Easter egg. I would rather go back to the orphanage than stay here another day.'

For once, Daisy Dashwood was lost for words.

Peach, Petal and Plum filed back into the lounge.

'Is there anything else you want us to do, Emily Vole?'

'Yes,' she said. 'Plug in the TV again, please.'

Daisy burst into tears and screamed. 'Play and run around like you used to, my cutiekins.'

The triplets said with one voice, 'We don't do that any longer, Mother.'

'It's Mum, you always called me Mum.'

Taking no notice whatsoever, the triplets did what Emily told them to do, then sat in a row next to her.

Daisy phoned Ronald. He rushed home, fearing the worst.

'What is it, Smoochikins?' he said, finding Daisy in the kitchen in tears.

'Emily's gone on strike and the girls have been snatched.'

'What?' said Ronald. He pulled out his mobile phone. 'We must call the police! Have you called the police?'

'No,' said Daisy, 'because the girls are mindless zombies.'

Ronald checked on his daughters. They were playing Snakes and Ladders in the lounge without a word being said between them. No fighting for the dice, no hair pulling, no shouts or screams. It was all very strange.

'How are my little cutiekins?' asked Ronald.

'Very well, Father,' they said together in the same dull voice.

Ronald thought they were downright spooky. He was

on his way back into the kitchen when the doorbell rang.

'Emily,' Ronald hissed to Daisy, which was the signal for Emily to be locked away in the laundry room. But his wife didn't move.

Ronald opened the door. There was no one there, or so he thought. Then he heard a voice say, 'Hello, I am Alfred Twizell of Alfred & Alfred Solicitors.'

Ronald stared down at a tiny man.

'Come again?' said Ronald.

'I am Alfred Twizell, Miss String's solicitor. May I come in?'

And before Ronald could work out if that was a good idea or not, Mr Twizell was walking towards the dining room as if he knew his way around the house.

'Smoochikins, we have a visitor,' called Ronald.

Mr Alfred Twizell had a kind, understanding face. He opened his briefcase and spread his papers out before him.

'I have come regarding the last will and testament of Miss Ottoline String,' he said to the startled Dashwoods.

'What's that got to do with us?' said Daisy.

'Nothing,' replied Mr Twizell. 'But it has everything to do with Emily Vole. It is Emily Vole who I am here to see.'

Chapter Ten

Emily was busy packing the few things she owned into the little cardboard suitcase. Her mind was made up. The minute the Dashwoods went to bed that night she would run away.

There was a knock on the laundry room door. Emily quickly hid her suitcase under a sheet.

'Come in,' she said. No one had ever been so polite as to knock before. Standing in a row were Peach, Petal and Plum.

'Mother and Father have a visitor,' they said. 'He wants to see you.'

That's a turn up for the books, thought Emily as she followed the three zombies into the dining room. Ronald Dashwood sounded angry.

'This is the stupidest thing I have ever heard. Why

would Miss String leave Emily all her worldly goods? She hardly knew the brat.'

Alfred Twizell stood up when Emily entered the room. He was about the same height as her, with white bushy eyebrows that framed a gentle face. He shook her hand.

'An honour to meet you at last, Miss Vole. Miss String and Fidget were very fond of you. It's such a sad time.'

'Where is Fidget?' asked Emily.

'Around and about,' said Mr Twizell. 'It's been a busy week, what with the funeral and one thing and another. It's all very discombobulating.'

'Come again?' said Daisy.

Alfred Twizell repeated the word. 'Dis-com-bob-u-lat-ing. It means unsettling.'

'Oh, my days! Why couldn't you just say that in the first place? Look here, Mr Whatever-your-tangled-up-name is, I'm telling you, Emily never even met the old . . .' Daisy stopped.

'You are wrong,' said Mr Twizell firmly.

He explained to Emily that Miss String's house and its contents were to be sold.

'All the money from the sale will be kept in a trust fund until you are eighteen. Of course, you can call on it sooner if there is an emergency.'

'Well, that's going to amount to nothing more than a bucket of pigs' tails,' said Daisy. 'The house is falling down and it's full of rubbish.'

'Sotheby's, the auctioneers from London, are there at the moment taking stock,' continued Mr Twizell.

'Of what?' said Daisy. 'A pile of old tat?'

Mr Twizell looked at Mrs Dashwood. 'That tat, as you call it, is priceless. Much of it will be going to museums and private collectors.'

Ronald coughed. His ears were beginning to turn even more red than usual.

'How much, exactly, is priceless? Are we talking *hundreds* of thousands?'

Mr Twizell ignored the question and addressed Emily. 'Miss String also left you a small shop.'

'A shop?' repeated Ronald. 'Are you a joker? Yes,

you are, aren't you? Haven't I've seen you on television? Smoochikins, he's just winding us up. You're from that programme – what's it called . . . I'm right, aren't I? This is a spoof.'

'No, it's not,' said Alfred Twizell.

'You can't be serious. The girl's too young to own a toothbrush,' said Ronald.

'But not too young,' replied Mr Twizell, 'to be your unpaid servant.'

'That's a bit strong,' said Ronald. 'We've done our very best by her, haven't we, Smoochikins? We adopted her out of the goodness of our hearts. It's not our fault she's as thick as a brick. She's away with the fairies, unteachable.'

'Balderdash,' said Mr Twizell. 'Miss String taught Miss Vole English, French, German, maths and history.'

'French? German?' said Daisy. 'Don't be daft.'

Mr Twizell said something to Emily in French.

'Je m'appelle Emily Vole,' she replied. 'Which means, "My name is Emily Vole."'

'You what?' said Daisy, flabbergasted.

Then Mr Twizell asked Emily another question, this time in German. Emily answered fluently, in a perfect German accent.

'Well, I never,' said Daisy. 'Does that gobbledygook make sense to you, Ronald?'

'Yes, Smoochikins,' Ronald said, astonished.

Mr Twizell finally spoke to Emily in Old English. He could tell by their puzzled faces that the Dashwoods hadn't a clue what he was saying. 'Fidget will wait for you tonight outside the laundry room window. You must get as far away from here as you can. Do you understand?' Emily nodded.

'You are in great danger,' said Alfred Twizell. 'There is not a moment to be lost.'

'Of course, Ronald and I will be looking after Emily's finances,' interrupted Daisy Dashwood. She smiled her sweetest smile, fluttering her false eyelashes at Alfred Twizell. 'That is, until she is eighteen.'

'You will be doing no such thing,' said Alfred Twizell, as he put the papers back into his briefcase. 'Neither of you will have any part of Emily's inheritance, Miss String has made sure of that.' Turning to Emily, he said, 'Miss Vole, I will be seeing you very soon.'

Emily and the Dashwoods followed him into the hall. Only then did Mr Twizell notice the three zombies, standing there, staring at nothing.

'May I ask, Mrs Dashwood . . . did a tall woman call here last week? A Ms Harper?'

'Yes, she was from–'

'I thought so,' said Alfred Twizell.

'What does that mean?' shrieked Daisy Dashwood into the oncoming night.

But Alfred Twizell had vanished.

Chapter Eleven

Daisy Dashwood was beside herself with rage. As soon as Alfred Twizell left, she grabbed Emily and gave her a sharp clip round the ear.

'You two-timing little minx,' she bellowed. 'Spreading lies. Learning rubbish. Inheriting shops. Behind our backs. After all we've done for you!'

'Now, steady on, Smoochikins,' interrupted Ronald, 'We don't want to be cross with Emily now, do we?'

'Why not?' asked Daisy, ready to give her another smack.

Ronald whispered to his wife.

Daisy gritted her teeth and let go of Emily.

'Sit down, Emily,' said Ronald in his hedge fund manager voice, slimy, slippery. 'You are a very lucky girl, aren't you, inheriting all that money – plus a shop? Of course, you are too young to know about investments and how to make your money grow. Never mind what Mr Twizell said, you will need some professional help and that's where I come in, as your adoptive father. Tomorrow we'll go and see my lawyer. If you do what he tells you, we might give you your old room back, mightn't we, Smoochikins?' Daisy pursed her thin red lips tighter than a drawstring bag. 'You would like that, wouldn't you, Emily? Perhaps you'd even go to school with other boys and girls.'

Emily could only think of Fidget waiting outside to help her run away. That thought alone made her feel brave.

'You were supposed to be my adoptive parents, you were supposed to care for me, you were supposed to send me to school even if I hadn't inherited a shop. I am not supposed to be your Cinderella. So buddleia to all your promises. I wouldn't trust you with a piggy bank if I had one.'

'You little minx! Oh, my days,' said Daisy. She stood bolt upright, looking like a man-eating boa constrictor.

She dragged Emily to the laundry room, while Emily fought with all her might to free herself. It was no use. Once again she was shut in the laundry room. The key turned in the door.

When everyone had gone to bed, Emily moved the ironing board to the window. She was relieved to find that the Dashwoods had forgotten to lock it. With her cardboard suitcase in one hand, she climbed out. Unfortunately, she missed her footing and by mistake landed on the dustbins outside. They clanged louder than a hundred alarm bells.

'That's blown it,' said a familiar voice and Fidget appeared from the bushes. They made a run for it.

'I'm so pleased you're here,' said Emily.

'I'm so pleased you're free, my little ducks. But you'll have to go faster than that.'

'I'm trying,' said Emily, 'but my slippers keep falling off.'

'Slippers,' said Fidget. He stopped and opened a

small rucksack he was carrying on his back. Emily was impressed to see how well dressed he was. In brogues, an overcoat, scarf and hat, he almost didn't look like a long-haired tortoiseshell cat, apart from his tail. He quickly took out a pair of Miss String's lace-up boots and a red coat. Both fitted Emily as if they had been made for her.

'Better?' asked Fidget.

'Better,' said Emily.

At that moment, the light went on in the Dashwoods' bedroom. The window opened and Ronald looked out. Emily and Fidget pressed themselves into the shadows of the squirrel cut hedges.

'What is it?' Emily heard Daisy ask.

'Only that huge cat from next door, I think.'

'Tomorrow,' screeched Daisy, 'come what may, I'm taking that mangy cat to the vet to be put down. I just wish we could do the same with . . .'

Fidget and Emily didn't wait to hear another word. They set off as fast as they could, paw in hand. They ran away from the executive houses, down the lane towards the woods. Beyond the woods lay the railway station.

Then they heard the sound of a car, speeding towards them.

Fidget pulled Emily behind a tree. The car's headlights lit up the woods and came to a grinding halt. Ronald and Daisy Dashwood climbed out.

'I thought I saw her, over there,' said Daisy.

Ronald shone a torch into the woods.

'There she is!' shouted Daisy. 'The little minx – she's with someone. Ronald – who's she with? I can't see.'

Ronald's torch shone blindly into the inky night. Fidget could see perfectly well in the dark, due to having cat's eyes. He nimbly guided Emily along the woodland path and across a small bridge, avoiding the boggy marsh that surrounded the stream.

On the other side they started to run again. Emily glanced back at the torchlight still close on their heels. Suddenly, Daisy screamed.

'Ronald, I'm stuck! Why didn't you tell me it was all boggy?'

Slurping sounds could be heard and Ronald cursed as he too slid into the marsh.

'Ronald,' Daisy bellowed. 'I have lost my thousand-pound shoes in all this mud. Oh, my days. That minx has had it when I lay my hands on her.'

'Do you know where we're going?' Emily asked Fidget anxiously.

'Yes, don't worry, my little ducks, I've done this many times before.'

'Run away?' asked Emily.

'No,' said Fidget. 'Gone travelling.'

They arrived at East Grimewood station with only moments to spare before their train arrived. Emily was flabbergasted that no one noticed Fidget was a cat. The ticket man didn't even look up as he asked for two first class tickets to London Liverpool Street. Once on board the train, Emily was certain they were safe. They had escaped by a whisker.

Chapter Twelve

Emily's heart sank as the Dashwoods rushed on to the platform, shouting at the conductor to stop the train.

'Get under the table,' said Fidget. He disappeared behind a newspaper he'd found lying on the seat next to him.

'What's happening?' asked Emily.

'The Dashwoods are wet through,' said Fidget under his breath. 'Mrs Dashwood has no shoes and Ronald's white trousers are poo-brown. He, too, is missing a shoe. The conductor is staring at them as if they are both bonkers.' Fidget chuckled. 'Now the station-master is leading them away.'

The whistle sounded and the train lurched forward.

'We're off,' said Fidget.

'Gosh,' said Emily, impressed. 'You really do know what to do.'

'Of course,' replied Fidget. 'Animal instinct.'

Emily returned to her seat, relieved to see the Dashwoods becoming a speck of dirt in the distance.

'Do you know why Alfred Twizell said I was in danger?'

'Yes. Because of Harpella,' replied Fidget.

'Who's she?' asked Emily.

'I believe she called herself Doris Harper when she paid a visit to your ex-adoptive-mother-stroke-employer Mrs Dashwood.'

'Oh, no!' said Emily.

'Oh, yes, my little ducks. Half bird, all witch, is Harpella. The scariest old trout who ever lived. It was she who snatched away the spirits of the triplets.'

'How?' said Emily.

'The same way she has always done such things – with her spirit lamp. I'll tell you this for a barrel-full of pickled herrings – that lamp has a lot to answer for. Harpella and her spirit lamp caused the accident that killed Miss String.'

Emily felt a lump of sadness in her throat.

'Is Harpella the same witch who killed the magician?' she asked.

'Yes, and she would kill you too if she could. She can't because you're human. But she'll try to trick you to get her hands on the keys. She's been after you since you broke the spell and brought the keys back to life. Now *you're* the Keeper of the Keys.'

'But why me?'

'Search my sardine tin, I don't know.'

The keys had climbed out of his rucksack and were dancing about on the table.

'Not this again,' said Fidget, trying to catch them. 'We don't want Harpella to hear them. The little blighters take no notice of me. They had me chasing my tail until I told them you were coming with us.'

Emily opened her small suitcase and the keys, all seventeen of them, their boots neatly tied, jumped in together. She firmly locked the clasp.

Fidget noticed tears in her eyes and put his paw

across the table. Emily held it tight.

'It's not your fault, my little ducks. No one, not even Miss String, could have guessed that it would be you who would wake up the keys.'

Emily stopped crying as the train was coming into London. That was when Fidget saw what he had been dreading. Heading his way, dressed in an ill-fitting train steward's uniform, her hair alight with flames and snakes, was Harpella. Her scrawny bird's talons clasped the handle of a tea trolley and peeping from under her skirt were her crimson chicken legs. She was throwing plastic cups at any passengers who were foolish enough to ask for refreshments, and if they complained she pelted them with chocolate bars and crisp packets.

Over the tannoy the conductor could be heard:

'If any off-duty policemen are on board, would they please make themselves known to the train staff immediately.'

Emily, who had never seen Harpella in the flesh, so to speak, couldn't mistake the unforgettable voice of Doris Harper. She peered round and nearly let out a scream. Harpella looked as though she had escaped from a horror film. Why Daisy Dashwood had been foolish enough to let her into the house in the first place, Emily couldn't understand.

At that moment the conductor rushed past them, heading for the fiery creature.

'I wouldn't,' said Fidget, putting out a paw to try to stop him. 'Best to let enraged witches be.'

'I have a duty towards my passengers,' said the conductor, and bravely barred Harpella's way.

'You can't come in here,' he said to her. 'These are first class coaches.'

'Time to leave,' said Fidget, and stood up. They walked swiftly to the front of the train.

Suddenly, there was a flash, as if it had been hit by a thunderbolt. The train shuddered to a violent halt, its brakes shrieking, its wheels grinding on the tracks. The first two carriages just reached the platform of Liverpool Street Station and miraculously, the doors flew open.

Emily looked back into the carriage to see a small pink rabbit hop-hop-hopping towards her.

'Tickets please,' he called out pitifully. 'Anyone with tickets?'

'Fidget, look, there's a pink rabbit. We can't just leave it.'

'Yes, we can,' said Fidget, who was already on the platform.

'I can't,' said Emily. 'The poor thing looks so sad.' She scooped it up and jumped off the train, her suitcase in one hand and the rabbit under her arm. She and Fidget ran as fast as they could through the main concourse.

The station clock showed midnight. The last train had just left and Liverpool Street Station was empty, apart from the police officers heading for the half-stranded train, their walkie-talkies blaring.

Emily followed Fidget along the side of Platform 10 to where the lost property office stood. It appeared, like everything else, to be closed. Fidget knocked on the door and it was opened by a young man with a ring in his nose and a Mohican hair style. A blue cockerel crest stuck up right along the middle of his head.

'You made it,' he said.

'Yes, Sam. It was touch and go.'

'Come in, come in,' said Sam. He shut and bolted the door behind them.

'Harpella, I take it,' said Sam. 'I've been watching the CCTV cameras – it doesn't look good.'

Emily stared at the monitor. The police were on the platform, which was filled with pink rabbits.

Sam looked down at the rabbit nibbling his trousers.

'This one?' asked Sam.

'The conductor of the train, unfortunately,' sighed Fidget. 'I tried to warn him.'

'Excuse me,' interrupted Emily. 'This rabbit is the conductor of the train?'

'Yes,' said Fidget. 'And most probably he has a wife and two carrots at home.'

'Harpella and the spirit lamp, then,' said Sam.

'Yes,' said Fidget.

'Oh dear.'

'Oh dear, indeed,' said Fidget.

'Tickets, please,' said the pink rabbit.

Chapter Thirteen

Emily had no idea how she and Fidget had arrived in the heart of the countryside. The last thing she remembered was the lost property office, and the next thing she knew she was standing in the early morning sunshine at a disused railway station.

'Come on, my little ducks,' said Fidget, leaping down from the platform on to the grassy tracks.

'Wait,' said Emily. 'Where's the pink rabbit?'

Fidget picked up a picnic hamper. Emily lifted the lid and peered in to see the rabbit munching on a carrot.

'Tickets, please,' he said.

'Luckily for us, someone had left this hamper in Lost Property.'

They set off, following the overgrown railway track. In the early morning mist a little town could be seen.

And beside the town ran a river, its boats twinkling silver in the glimmering sunlight.

'It looks like a picture postcard,' said Emily. Her tummy rumbled.

'Hungry?' asked Fidget.

'Yes,' said Emily. And she was.

Fidget opened his rucksack and rummaged inside until he found what he was searching for. He pulled out an argumentative kettle, who in its turn pulled out a tea cup. The tea cup pulled out its friend and two saucers, while the milk jug and the sugar bowl played tug-of-war with a spotted tablecloth.

'They were much better behaved when Miss String was alive,' said Fidget sadly, bringing out a bag of buns, a packet of butter and a pot of strawberry jam.

'Maybe they miss her like we do.'

'That's a good enough reason in my litter tray,' said Fidget. 'The trouble is, I don't quite have the same sparkle as the old girl when it comes to controlling magic.'

A fight had started between the milk jug and the tea pot.

'I always go first,' said the milk jug. 'Remember? Milk first, then tea.'

'Stop it, all of you,' said Emily firmly. 'Just be good. What would Miss String say if she were here?'

At that all the china stood to attention.

'Thank you,' said Emily. 'We have quite enough trouble without you all being difficult.'

'Well put, my little ducks,' said Fidget, impressed.

Emily drank her tea and ate her bun with the delicious strawberry jam.

'Can I ask you a question?' she said.

'Just one. I'm not Miss String, I'm a cat whose mind is on fish paste.' One question. That, thought Emily was going to be very hard indeed. There were so many questions she wanted to ask. Like how had they arrived here when last night they were in London? Instead, she settled on: 'What is a spirit lamp?'

'It's a magic lamp that Harpella stole from a wizard a long time ago.'

'What for?'

'Hold your whiskers, I'm working up to that point. To catch fairies.'

'That's terrible!' said Emily.

'Diabolical, that's what Miss String called it. Diabolical.'

'Whatever it means, I agree,' said Emily.

'It means, according to Miss String, about the worst thing you could ever see,' continued Fidget. 'Harpella had a mission to murder each and every one of the fairies in the world.'

'How?' asked Emily.

'That's another question.'

'No, it's not, it's joined up to the first.'

Fidget thought for a long time. 'You're right.' He took a deep breath. 'The spirit lamp gives off a light that is impossible to resist. The fairy is sucked into the flame, like a moth. Swat – gone.'

'That's dia-*bol*-ical!' said Emily.

'It was, until one midsummer, all the fairies who were left in England met and decided their wings should be locked away so they would no longer be tempted to fly into the spirit lamp. That was when they asked for the help of the magician . . .'

'The magician who designed Wings & Co?' interrupted Emily. 'The shop with the legs . . .'

'The very same,' said Fidget. 'And he had some curious cabinets built for the fairies' wings, and put a spell on the keys to them so the wings would be safe. It took a lot of craftsmanship to build those curious cabinets,' he added with pride.

'You were the Master Builder Miss String told me about, weren't you?' said Emily.

'I might have been,' said Fidget, gathering up the remaining cup and saucer.

'And it was Harpella who turned you into a cat, wasn't it?' she asked.

'That,' said Fidget, 'is clearly two more questions.'

Emily stood up and brushed the crumbs off her coat.

'That's the trouble with questions,' she said. 'One is never enough.'

'Personally, I find the same with a good kipper,' replied Fidget, putting the china and the kettle back in the rucksack. He picked up the hamper containing the pink rabbit. 'Come on, my little ducks,' he said. 'We have to find the shop.'

'Why do we have to find the shop?'

'Because there are a few fairies out there who are desperate for their wings.'

'But if the keys open the cabinets and the fairies get their wings back, won't Harpella just kill them like before?'

'That's why she wants the keys, my little ducks, and that's why we also have to find the old witch and take that lamp away from her. But it's not going to be that easy. She has other powers, just as diabolical.'

'How do you catch a witch?' said Emily.

'How do you catch a fish?' replied Fidget. 'With bait. And that's what we're going to do.'

'Oh dear,' said Emily. 'I don't like the sound of that.'

Chapter Fourteen

Emily began to think they might never find the shop. Podgy Bottom wasn't a large town and it seemed to be stuffed full of antique shops and very little else.

'Not even a fishmonger,' Fidget said bitterly. 'And definitely not our shop. I think Alfred Twizell was wrong about this. The shop has gone walking again.'

'If only we had an address – or some sort of clue,' said Emily, thinking of the old lady detective with the knitting. 'Anyway,' she added, 'why would a building hide?'

'Harpella?' suggested Fidget. 'A good enough reason in my litter tray.'

As instructed, Emily held tightly to the keys. According to Fidget, the minute they were near the shop the keys would spring into action. So far, they had been round the town twice and the keys had not sprung.

It was mid-morning and for the third time that day they were standing by the forlorn statue of Queen Victoria.

'What now?' asked Emily.

'I don't rightly know,' said Fidget. 'Miss String had the brains, I have the brawn.'

They set off again, this time up a narrow lane that led away from the town square. A placard outside a newsagent read, 59 PEOPLE VANISH ON MIDNIGHT TRAIN.

'It's in the papers, then,' said Emily.

'Yes, but fortunately nothing about pink rabbits,' said Fidget.

'Tickets, please,' said the mournful voice from the basket.

Farther along the street was a junk shop. Outside it had a few chairs, an old mangle and boxes of odd china plates. Suddenly the keys came to life, wriggling around with such urgency that the ring that held them together gave way in Emily's hands.

'Oh, look!' said Emily, as the keys jumped to the ground and ran as fast as their booted feet would let them towards the junk shop.

Fidget peered through the window as the keys kicked at his brogues.

'No. This is most definitely not our shop. I don't know what those keys are up to,' said Fidget. 'Blast my whiskers! First the kettle, now the keys. Why can't anything behave?'

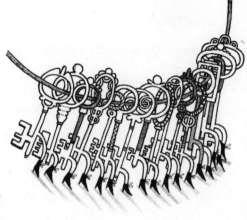

One of the keys stopped kicking him, and for a non-speaking piece of ironmongery seemed to be saying quite a lot.

'Maybe we should go in?' suggested Emily.

'Maybe,' said Fidget and pushed open the door. 'I bet this is a red herring,' he muttered to himself as the shop bell rang.

Inside, the light was very dim and the shop smelled of old books and mothballs. Emily could see a stuffed alligator, a tailor's dummy, saucepans, gas lamps, a skull, and a gramophone with a stack of records. But the object that immediately caught her eye sat on a round table in a Victorian birdcage. It was a figurine of a handsome young fellow wearing an old-fashioned frock coat. For a doll he was extraordinarily lifelike, with silvery-blue glass eyes that appeared to twinkle. He had floppy, auburn hair and long, elegant hands.

Emily had never seen anything so beautiful before. She wanted to buy the doll, free it from its prison bars and take it away with her. Emily studied the little fellow for so long that she was certain she saw his lips move.

'Hello, can I help you?' said a voice behind her. Emily spun round to find a teenaged boy standing there, a college scarf wound around his neck.

'Just looking,' said Fidget. 'You have an interesting collection.'

'Not me, my grandpa. I just help out in the hols. Wowza,' he said. 'That is one ace catsuit, dude.'

'Thanks,' said Fidget.

The keys had hidden under the round table.

Emily pulled on Fidget's sleeve. 'Can we buy that?' she asked, pointing at the birdcage and quite forgetting why they were there.

'No,' said Fidget. 'We are not here to buy . . .' He stopped and stared at the birdcage. 'Buster . . .' he said, stepping forwards and knocking into a glass display cabinet. 'It can't be.'

The student rushed to catch the case before it toppled over altogether.

'Sorry, mate,' said Fidget.

'Gramps has so much stuff in here,' the student said as he put the cabinet back in its place. 'It's almost impossible to move. I like the way your tail swishes and curls into a question mark just like a real cat's. Do you do it by remote control?'

'No, you don't,' said Fidget absently. He was still staring at the little fellow in the birdcage. 'Is this for sale?'

'Yep, I think so. I'll go and check.'

With that the student disappeared behind a curtain at the back of the shop.

'Twiddle my whiskers and call me tuna,' said Fidget.

Just then, the figure started to wave its arms.

Emily looked at it in amazement.

'He's alive!' she said. 'Oh, no, that's terrible! We must free him.'

'Yes, yes, we must. Oh dear, oh dear, what a pickle,' said Fidget.

'Do you know who it is?' asked Emily.

'Know who it is?' repeated Fidget. 'Yes, of course I know who it is. It's Buster. Buster Ignatius Spicer, one of Wings & Co's great fairy detectives!'

'A detective?' said Emily. 'Miss String never said anything about detectives.'

'She couldn't – secret stuff and all that fishpaste.'

'What is he doing in there?' asked Emily.

'A good question, my little ducks, a good question indeed.'

Fidget was trying to open the cage when the student came back.

'Sorry, dude,' he said cheerfully. 'That item's not for sale. Gramps has had it for years. It would take a lot of money to make him part with it.'

Chapter Fifteen

The receptionist at the Red Lion Hotel wore a well-rehearsed smile along with the badge pinned to her jacket. It read 'Joan' and underneath 'Receptionist'.

'Sorry,' said Joan, smiling. 'We don't allow pets. It's company policy.'

'I'm not a pet,' said Fidget. 'Do I look like a pet?'

'You look like a very large cat and, as I said, we don't take animals.'

Fidget leaned forward and whispered, 'If you must know, I have a medical condition which means I can only go out dressed as a cat. I am, as you can imagine, somewhat sensitive on the subject.'

Joan looked genuinely shocked and the well-rehearsed smile crumbled into concern.

'Crikey. I didn't mean to be rude. That's awful.'

109

'I know,' said Fidget, suitably wounded.

'Sorry . . . it's just that the cat disguise looks so real.'

'I know; it happens all the time. We need two rooms.'

Joan, still bright red, said, 'We have a very nice suite on the second floor. It's rather expensive but it does have two bedrooms and an interconnecting lounge.'

'We'll take it,' said Fidget, handing Emily the fat brown envelope Alfred Twizzel had given him.

Emily carefully counted out the twenty-pound notes, just as she had in the junk shop.

'One thousand pounds?' The young man had been taken aback by the sum on offer. 'Wowza! One thousand pounds for a Victorian birdcage?'

And that is how Fidget and Emily came to be standing in the foyer of the Red Lion Hotel in Podgy Bottom with a rucksack, a cardboard suitcase, a picnic hamper and a rather badly wrapped birdcage.

It was only after a waiter had delivered a tray of delicious food to their suite that Buster Ignatius Spicer climbed gloomily out of the birdcage. Small and dejected, he sat down on the floor, his head in his hands, his legs stretched out before him.

'I let Miss String down and now that enchanting lady is dead. It was up to me to protect her from Harpella and I didn't.'

'How do you know she's dead?' asked Emily, feeding some rocket salad to the rabbit.

'Because Fidget would be with Miss String if she was still alive,' said Buster.

'Eat something,' said Fidget.

'I can't,' said Buster sulkily. 'It's all too big. But I would very much like to meet the wizard who broke the spell the magician put on the keys.'

'You have,' said Fidget. 'She's sitting right next to you. Emily is the new Keeper and now Harpella is after her.'

'You?' said Buster to Emily. 'You? But you're a girl! Not a wizard, not even a fairy.'

'And who are *you*, exactly?' asked Emily.

'Miss String must have told you about me,' said Buster.

'No,' said Emily firmly. 'She didn't.'

'Perhaps you weren't listening. Well, I will tell you again. My best friend and I ran a detective agency.'

'Where?' asked Emily.

'In Miss String's shop,' Buster said impatiently.

'But Miss String told me the shop sold potions and such things.'

'That was before I took over. My friend was twelve, one year older than the age I am now. We made a good team. We found and returned what was lost or stolen, captured the thieves, freed the innocent. That's the general gist. Then without any warning the Fairy Wars started.'

'Miss String never told me about the Fairy Wars, or about you. Or about the detective agency. I wouldn't have forgotten. Who started the Fairy Wars?' asked Emily.

'Harpella,' said Buster, 'with the spirit lamp.'

'Why? How?' asked Emily.

'Don't you know anything? The human world used to protect us, as we did them. Over time, fewer people believed in us and as our power became weaker

Harpella's became stronger.'

'But why did she want to kill all the fairies?'

'She married one and then he ran off and left her,' said Buster.

'In other words,' said Fidget, 'it's personal. A family problem for which all the fairies have been made to pay.'

'What happened to Harpella's husband?'

'Excuse my asking,' said Buster, 'but is she always like this? Full of *why*s and *how*s and *where*s?'

'Yep,' said Fidget.

'So are all the fairies in the spirit lamp?' asked Emily.

'I wish,' said Buster.

'No,' said Fidget. 'They are not. Once a fairy is dead, he or she is gone. Nothing will bring them back.'

'Harpella is up to her old tricks again, isn't she?' said Buster, looking cautiously at the pink rabbit, which seemed enormous to him.

'Spot on the sprat,' said Fidget. 'She changed a whole train full of passengers into pink bunny rabbits in the hope of catching my little ducks. We had a lucky escape.'

Buster leaned on the birdcage. 'Did Harpella see you

get off the train?'

'No,' said Fidget. 'She was too busy.'

'Well, that's one bit of good news,' said Buster. 'That means she thinks you are among the pink rabbits, and that means we have a head start on her.'

'Well, twiddle my whiskers and call me haddock! I hadn't thought of that,' said Fidget.

'If we can find the shop, I can get my wings back,' said Buster.

'But first we need to get the lamp, otherwise you're a fairy fishcake.'

Chapter Sixteen

The *Daily Bugle* reported that the fate of the fifty-nine passengers was the biggest mystery of all time. An eye-witness claimed to have seen a flying saucer hovering above the train. There was even a man who posted fuzzy pictures on YouTube claiming they showed a witch on a broomstick who had swooped down and turned the passengers into pink rabbits. No one believed a word of it.

Ronald and Daisy Dashwood knew that Emily must be among the fifty-nine. Not that they were sad about it. In fact, it couldn't be a better outcome. 'You know what this means, Smoochikins?' said Ronald.

'No,' said Daisy. 'What?'

'It means that we, as Emily's legal guardians, will have access to all that money she inherited from Miss String.'

'But we haven't reported her missing, have we?' said Daisy.

It was the station-master at East Grimewood who told the police that only two passengers had boarded the train on that particular evening. One a gent, the other a little girl in a red coat.

'Then there was this loony couple. They dashed on to the platform just before the whistle blew, saying their daughter was on the train,' said the station-master. 'I thought they were off their rockers. Both covered in mud and the woman had no shoes on.'

James Cardwell, a senior detective at Scotland Yard, went to interview the Dashwoods. He had been in the police force for as long as anyone could remember. His age and length of service were lost in the mists of time. He had a reputation for solving difficult cases and Operation Bunny was certainly a difficult case.

Detective Cardwell was immediately suspicious of the

Dashwoods. As he listened to Ronald and Daisy's story, he knew something was wrong with this picture of a happy family.

'We were just too upset,' explained Daisy. 'I mean, she was such a darling daughter to us.'

'Although she did have special needs, due to being abandoned in a hatbox,' added Ronald.

'Even more reason to report her missing straight away, surely,' said Detective Cardwell, unimpressed by Daisy batting her false eyelashes.

While she burbled on, Detective Cardwell remembered the letter he had received from his aunt about the little baby found in a hatbox at Stansted Airport.

And this whining woman and her red-eared husband had been allowed to adopt the baby. The name Ronald Dashwood had a familiar ring to it – for all the wrong reasons, of that Detective Cardwell was certain. He asked to see Emily's bedroom and was shown to the spare room. It was then he saw the three little girls standing all together on the landing. He looked at his notes.

'Your daughters?' he asked Daisy.

'Yes, Peach, Petal and Plum,' she said.

'And they do advertising work?'

'No,' said Daisy with a genuine gulp of emotion. 'No, not since . . .'

'. . . since Ms Harper came to see us,' said the triplets in one eerie voice.

Detective Cardwell crouched to their level. Their blank faces confirmed all he had suspected.

'Did Ms Harper have anything with her when she came to see you?'

'Yes,' said the girls. 'A brand new designer handbag.'

'Do you remember what was in the handbag?'

'A lamp,' they said. 'It had rainbow-coloured light and we followed the light.'

'That's very good,' said Detective Cardwell. 'Where did you follow it to?'

'Into the lamp,' they all said together. 'That's where we are.'

'Do you miss your big sister?' asked Detective Cardwell, changing the subject.

'No,' said the triplets. 'She was just our nanny. Mother

misses not having a servant to push around. Mother is going to kill Emily Vole when she comes home. It was Emily Vole's fault Mother ruined a pair of thousand-pound shoes.'

'Shut up, the three of you,' screeched Daisy. 'Just shut up!'

'Why did Emily run away, Mrs Dashwood?' Detective Cardwell asked her for the second time.

'I don't know.'

'Yes, you do,' chorused the little girls.

'Mr Dashwood,' said Detective Cardwell, turning to Ronald, 'am I right in thinking you have some connection with Sprout Securities in Brussels?'

Ronald's ears began to go even redder.

'I think we should have our lawyer here before we answer any more questions,' he said.

James Cardwell left the Dashwoods' executive home and went next door to Miss String's house. He stood outside, feeling overcome with sadness. He had often visited Aunt Ottoline when he was a boy. It was here he had first met the remarkable Buster Ignatius Spicer.

A golden time. Buster was just a year younger than him, and all they had wanted was to be detectives. Aunt Ottoline, bless her cotton socks, had thought it a champion idea.

At first it was a bit of a lark, but the whole thing turned very nasty indeed. The battle with Harpella and the spirit lamp had been as good as lost. So many fairies were dead. It had been Buster's idea that all the remaining fairies hand in their wings. Reluctantly, James, like the other fairies, had given his wings to Buster to be locked away by the magician. After the magician's death Aunt Ottoline had hidden the keys. But he and the rest of the fairies had lost their magic, joined human time, grown up and grown tired of waiting for a new Keeper of the Keys to appear. As the centuries passed, hope had faded. The remaining fairies would have to live without their wings, forever stuck between two worlds.

He closed the front gate with a sigh and returned to his car. He hadn't seen Buster since just before the Battle of Waterloo. What if he had been murdered, like Aunt Ottoline? It was too terrible to think about.

Detective Cardwell started the engine. The fairy who'd walked out on Harpella had a lot to answer for.

Chapter Seventeen

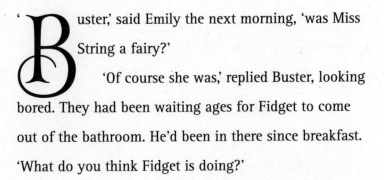

'Buster,' said Emily the next morning, 'was Miss String a fairy?'

'Of course she was,' replied Buster, looking bored. They had been waiting ages for Fidget to come out of the bathroom. He'd been in there since breakfast. 'What do you think Fidget is doing?'

'I don't know,' said Emily. 'Cats like to be clean.'

'But they hate water,' said Buster.

'I didn't think Miss String was a fairy,' said Emily, 'because she was the same size as all of us.'

'What makes you think fairies are small?'

'In fairy stories,' said Emily, 'you are all small.'

'Who wrote the stories?' asked Buster, tying his shoe laces.

'Lots of different writers, some from a very long

time ago.'

'Any of them fairies?' asked Buster.

'No. Don't be silly.'

'Exactly. Have you noticed how few fairies there are in those stories?' asked Buster. 'More often, there are hard-done-by princesses dressed in rags, and boring princes being all soppy. The only time we fairies come into the picture is when we are invited to christenings and grant daft wishes.'

Emily had to admit that Buster had a good point.

'Don't worry,' said Buster. 'The mistake you make is a common one. Fairies happen to have the gift of becoming smaller when necessary, which is handy. That's if you can resize yourself afterwards.'

'Which *you* can't.'

'YES-I-KNOW. A goblin I had a run-in with took that power away from me.'

Emily smiled to herself, and sat down, nibbling a piece of leftover toast.

'I can't understand why the keys took a shine to you. You, of all people,' said Buster. 'Perhaps it's because you are a human. The keys wouldn't be safe in fairy hands. That's why Miss String kept them hidden in the attic.'

'Until we had our history lessons,' said Emily.

'I don't suppose she thought anything would happen,' said Buster. 'After all, you are just a human girl, nothing to write to the Faerie Queene about.'

Emily was fed up with Buster. He was so rude and unpleasant.

'If you're so clever, how did you come to be trapped in a birdcage?'

Buster went as red as Ronald Dashwood's ears.

'I don't want to talk about it,' he said.

Ha, thought Emily, I'll come back to that one day.

'I hope you stay small forever and ever,' she said, and turned on the television.

The top story that morning on the local news network was the mysterious demolition of Arty McDuff's junk shop in Brittle Street, Podgy Bottom. The street where the junk shop had stood was cordoned off with police tape, and officers were turning onlookers away.

Emily and Buster stared open-mouthed at the TV.

'That's the shop we rescued you from,' said Emily.

'Enough of the rescue,' said Buster.

'Enough of me not being a fairy,' said Emily.

'Deal,' said Buster.

'The police cannot yet confirm,' the news reporter was saying, 'the cause of the explosion.'

'Crumbs,' said Buster. 'That's bad.'

Fidget appeared from the bathroom in a cloud of steam, his fur gleaming, his teeth shining bright.

'What have you been doing in there?' said Buster, turning to look at him.

'Grooming. Fur balls can be very uncomfortable,' said Fidget indignantly. 'Of course, you wouldn't understand, on account of having no fur.'

'Look,' said Emily, pointing to the TV.

Fidget stared at the screen. 'Well, smack me with a kipper and call me haddock, isn't that the junk shop we—'

'Yes!' Emily and Buster interrupted.

'Oh dear, oh dear,' said Fidget. 'This doesn't look too dandy.'

'Do you think,' said Emily, 'that *our* shop is all right?'

'I hope so. Come on,' said Fidget. 'Leave the rabbit here. This can only be the work of one person.'

'Harpella. I knew it,' said Buster. 'She must have worked out that you're not among the bunnies.' He climbed into Fidget's rucksack. 'Let's go and investigate.'

Down in the foyer they were stopped by the hotel manager.

'Excuse me, sir,' he said, 'but my colleague did tell you we don't allow pets.'

'Yes,' said Fidget, looking around anxiously.

'You have a rabbit in your room, sir, and that is not allowed.'

'He's a dwarf,' said Fidget. 'A relative of mine with the same condition as me, except he thinks he is a ticket collector.'

'I'm afraid,' said the manager, 'I'm very much afraid . . .'

'With good reason,' replied Fidget, as the dreadful apparition of Harpella burst through the doors of the hotel.

There wasn't a moment to lose. Fidget and Emily threw themselves into the lift. Fidget's rucksack was trapped in the lift doors and Emily had to use all her strength to free it. The thunderbolt had already struck the foyer as the lift doors closed.

Chapter Eighteen

Once back in the suite, Emily didn't waste a moment. She knew what had to be done. The keys had chosen her to be their keeper for a reason. She could feel them wriggling around in her pocket, eager to find the shop with the cabinets full of fairy wings. Leaving Fidget to retrieve Buster from the rucksack, she gingerly climbed out of the window and ran down the fire-escape.

The keys were nudging and pushing her along. There was no doubt they knew where they were going. Back along the small high street she went, into the square with the statue of Queen Victoria. It was quite easy to see how they had missed the shop. It was simple. Yesterday, it hadn't been there. Today, there it stood, an old crooked building with a crooked chimney. It looked just as Emily

had imagined it would from the stories Miss String had told her. The top windows were leaning forward trying to catch sight of their belly button bow windows. In one of them a sign read CLOSED.

Emily's heart started to beat faster. Something wasn't right. The door was hanging loose on its hinges. The keys had stopped moving, they had turned to cold iron again in her pocket.

It struck Emily that the shop was doing its level best to hold something or someone in. Then she caught a glimpse of a face at one of the top windows and a long, claw-like painted fingernail click-click-clicking on the window pane. Harpella had broken into the shop. She was one step closer to getting her talons on the fairy wings.

Emily didn't need to see any more. She turned and ran as fast as her legs would carry her all the way back to the Red Lion Hotel. She arrived, completely out of breath, to see three fire engines, two police cars and an ambulance in front of the hotel, all their lights flashing. Emily walked round to the back of the building and climbed up the fire escape to the suite. Now she knew where the shop was, and Harpella was locked inside. The Keeper of the Keys had a plan.

Chapter Nineteen

James Cardwell had had a busy morning. He had been out to the top secret military research laboratory in Hendon where the pink rabbits from the train were being held. Every one of the rabbits was housed in its own cage, with fresh straw and carrots.

The army officer in charge of Operation Bunny told Cardwell that they had shown no signs of becoming human again.

'Each rabbit has only one sentence,' he said. 'Each one different to all the others.'

Detective Cardwell walked up and down the line of caged rabbits.

One said, 'I'm on the train, dear, I can't speak now.'

Another said, 'I missed the 7.40 so I'm running late.'

Another, 'Yes, I love you too.'

The lab technician shrugged his shoulders.

'You can see what we're up against,' he said. 'It's impossible to identify them.'

'I wouldn't bother,' said Detective Cardwell. 'No one is going to be that pleased to hear his or her beloved has been turned into a pink rabbit.'

'What are we going to do with them?' said the army officer.

'Keep them safe until I solve this case.'

The army officer followed Detective Cardwell to his car. 'Have you any idea who is behind this?'

'Yes, but nothing I can share with you at present.'

As James Cardwell drove away he remembered being taken by Aunt Ottoline to the Great Exhibition in Hyde Park in 1851. At the time he had been fascinated by the dodo. The day they visited he had been bitterly disappointed to find that not only was it extinct but that the entire bird section had been closed to the public. Aunt Ottoline had been very anxious to get away.

'Why?' he had asked.

It was the only time he'd ever heard her say,

'Because. Just because.'

To compensate for not seeing the dodo she had promised him tea and cakes. As they left, park keepers with nets were trying to catch the dozens of orange rabbits that sat nibbling the grass.

His mobile rang. He was to go straightaway to the Red Lion Hotel in the town of Podgy Bottom. There had been another serious incident relating to Operation Bunny.

James Cardwell put on his blue light and drove at great speed out of London. He arrived at the hotel to find it cordoned off and the police looking uneasy. The constable in charge followed Detective Cardwell into the foyer. It was empty apart from two purple rabbits.

One said, 'Pets aren't allowed. It's hotel policy.'

The other said, 'This is the Red Lion Hotel, how can I help you?'

'We think it's the manager and the receptionist. She's called Joan.'

'Well, you'd better catch them before they hop off,' said Detective Cardwell.

'Yes, sir,' said the constable. He looked very nervous indeed. 'They won't bite, will they, sir?'

'I don't suppose so,' said Detective Cardwell. Studying the register he saw the name Mr Fidget. 'Are these the only guests staying here?'

'Yes. We haven't investigated their suite yet. We thought we should wait until you came. We're slightly worried that they too might have been . . . well, you know, rabbitified.'

The lift wasn't working so Detective Cardwell walked up the stairs and knocked on the door to the suite. It was opened by a girl in a red coat holding a tiny purple rabbit. He guessed straightaway from the description he'd received that this was Emily Vole. At least she was all right.

'I am Detective Cardwell,' he said. 'May I come in?'

Fidget was standing in front of a long mirror.

'l have a rabbit's tail. It's pink and ridiculous, look.'

'Hello, Fidget. Better to have the tail than be changed completely into a rabbit,' said the detective.

'Well, hook me a cod fish-finger!' said Fidget, spinning round. 'If it isn't little Jimmy Cardwell.'

'Little?' interrupted Emily. 'There's nothing little about the detective.'

James Cardwell laughed. 'When I knew Fidget I was little, but I have grown up. I'm just the same but older. Fidget, if you don't mind my asking, what is Emily Vole doing here?'

'Emily,' said Fidget proudly, 'is the new Keeper of the Keys.'

'How did that happen?' said Detective Cardwell, looking closely at Emily.

'I'll tell you later,' said Fidget.

Detective Cardwell dropped his gaze to the small purple rabbit Emily was holding. 'Who was that, then?'

'This is Buster,' said Emily.

'Are you sure?' said Detective Cardwell.

As if to prove the point, the rabbit said, 'I am Buster Ignatius Spicer.'

'He must have been struck before I was able to free the rucksack from the lift doors,' said Emily.

'Does he say anything else?' asked Detective Cardwell.

'No, thank goodness,' said Emily. 'He's very full of his name, which is long and quite hard to spell.'

Detective Cardwell laughed. 'No change there, then.'

He saw there was another rabbit, larger and pink, hopping about. 'Tickets, please,' it said.

'The train conductor,' explained Fidget. 'Emily rescued him.'

James Cardwell sat down heavily in an armchair.

'It's Harpella, isn't it?'

'Yes,' said Emily. 'She has a spirit lamp and this is what she likes to do best, change people into rabbits.'

'Except for the Dashwood triplets,' said Fidget, 'who she zombified rather than bunnified.'

'Look,' said Emily, sitting down. 'I have a plan.'

Fidget and James stared at her.

'A plan, James, she has a plan,' said Fidget proudly.

'You can see why your Aunt Ottoline chose to leave the shop to Emily.'

'His aunt?' said Emily, taken aback. She turned to James. 'Your aunt? Oh no, that means you are . . .'

'A fairy,' said James Cardwell. 'A fairy who handed in his wings to the detective agency and has been stuck at fifty for as long as he can remember.'

'Oh, dear,' said Emily, 'and there was I thinking you might be able to help me with my plan. I mean, I must have someone to distract Harpella while I try to grab the lamp. Now, who else could help? It has to be a human because Harpella can't kill humans, only change them into bunnies – and zombies of course . . . oh!' Emily jumped up. 'I have it! My ex-adoptive-mother-stroke-employer. She's fierce and frightening and she would do anything to have the triplets de-zombified.' She paused. 'Only I don't want to ever go back and live with her again.'

'You won't,' said Detective Cardwell. 'I give you my word.'

Chapter Twenty

Ever since the interview with Detective Cardwell, the Dashwoods had been as jumpy as a couple of crickets.

'Ronald,' whined Daisy, 'you're not in any trouble, are you?' Her gold card had been refused at Fancy Pants Boutique. 'I mean, we have a million in the bank, don't we?'

Ronald didn't answer. He was grey, only his ears remained red and one of them was stuck to his mobile phone.

'I'm busy, Smoochikins.'

'But, Ronald . . .'

'You're just going to have to cut back a bit, that's all. STOP SPENDING!' he shouted.

Never, in twelve years of marriage, had Ronald ever raised his voice to Daisy. Not once.

'You don't love me any more!' she screeched.

The land-line rang.

'Later, Smoochikins, later,' said Ronald, going into his study and closing the door.

Daisy let out a high-pitched scream. Ronald quickly reappeared.

'Look, I didn't mean to . . . oh,' he said, seeing his three daughters standing in a row like clockwork dolls.

'They gave me a terrible fright, that's all,' said Daisy.

'They give me the creeps,' said Ronald, returning to his call and shutting the door again.

The zombies smiled. Everything they did was in perfect unison.

'Father,' they said, 'is up to his neck in horse poo.'

'That's not a nice way to speak about your daddy.'

'You see, Mother dear,' they all said, 'the truth is, his money isn't his money, it's other people's money.'

'You what?' said Daisy, staring open-mouthed. 'You've lost me.'

'It's simple, Mother dearest. Unless Father can wash all the horse poo off him, he will never smell of roses.'

'You're talking double-dutch. I don't understand a blooming word. Oh, my days, why should this be happening to me? Me, of all people,' she cried. 'Me, who has always been so kind, so generous, to everyone.'

'Not to Emily Vole,' said the triplets. 'Remember? You want to kill her when she comes home.'

Daisy ran to her bedroom.

The zombies looked at one another and smiled again.

That evening, Daisy found Ronald packing a suitcase with files and computer disks and little else.

'Where are you going?' wailed Daisy. 'You can't leave me.'

'I have an important business meeting in Brussels,' said Ronald. 'A private plane is going to pick me up.'

'Can't I come with you?'

'No,' said Ronald firmly. He was on all fours, feeling under the bed.

'What are you looking for?' asked Daisy.

'Nothing,' said Ronald. 'There was a shoe box under here – you haven't moved it, have you?'

'No. Why would you keep a shoe box under the bed

when we have two walk-in wardrobes?'

Ronald didn't reply. He looked at his watch and tried to shut the suitcase.

'Please,' said Daisy. 'Please may I come with you?'

'No, you can't. Someone has to look after the children.'

'They aren't our girls,' wept Daisy. 'They're ruddy zombies.'

'That's not my fault,' said Ronald. 'You should never have let that Doris woman into the house.'

'So I'm to blame? Oh, my days, don't you want to help find out where our daughters are?'

'They're right outside, listening to every word we're saying. Now, Smoochikins, be good, I'll be back soon.'

The zombies were lined up by the front door, waiting for their father to come down the stairs.

'Goodbye, Father,' they said. Ronald ignored them and made a dash for the waiting car.

'Ronald!' Daisy cried. But Ronald and the car were just a blur of tail lights.

Very early the next morning there was a loud knock on the Dashwoods' executive front door.

The triplets, who hardly ever slept these days, had been up since crow's fart playing Scrabble. They answered the door to find several police officers standing there, all wearing bullet-proof vests. Among them was a very elegant young woman. She flashed her badge at the zombies. It said 'Fraud Squad'.

'Hello, I'm Penny. Are your mummy and daddy here?'

'Father ran away last night,' said the zombies.

'Can we come in?' asked Penny.

The little girls showed no signs of emotion when, a few minutes later, their mother was brought down the stairs screaming.

'I can't leave my darlings – what will they do without me?'

'What we always do, Mother dearest,' said the triplets, and they waved a cheerful goodbye to her.

Penny was about to ring the Social Services' child protection team when she felt a little hand resting on her back. She turned round to see the three girls standing there.

'If you want us to help you we suggest you put down the phone.'

Penny thought these children were most decidedly weird. More than weird, they looked zombified.

'If you let us stay here,' they said, 'we will give you the shoe box you are looking for. If you call Social Services, we won't. We will just pretend we don't know what you are talking about. After all, we are only little children.'

Penny felt a shiver go down her spine. Feebly, she agreed and the girls went to fetch the shoe box that Father had been so keen to take with him.

Daisy Dashwood sat in the police car, handcuffed to a woman police officer who turned up after the Fraud Squad had left. That nosy copper Cardwell had sent for her. She was still in her dressing-gown and, to add insult to injury, they hadn't even let her put on her war paint. She hadn't slept a wink, worried sick as she was about Ronald. She had tried his mobile phone about a thousand times but there was no answer. And those creepy little girls most definitely weren't her babies. Her babies had been snatched from her.

If that Doris woman is responsible, I will blooming well kill her when I next lay eyes on her, thought Daisy Dashwood, as the police car, light flashing, sped up the motorway towards the Red Lion Hotel.

Chapter Twenty-One

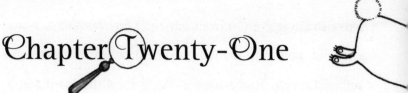

Detective James Cardwell often pondered the folly of human beings, especially the ones who called themselves grown-ups. Grown-up human beings didn't believe in fairies. Instead they watched horror films, and scared themselves witless with zombies and vampires. Why, he hadn't a clue. After all, he had been around for hundreds of years and had yet to meet a vampire or, for that matter, a werewolf. But a bad fairy or a goblin – well, that was something else altogether. Then there was Harpella, the queen of witches. The one thing he knew for certain was that she alone could cause more trouble than any grisly ghosty he had seen on TV.

When Daisy Dashwood arrived at the Red Lion Hotel later that morning, the place was still in chaos. Daisy, however, seemed quite unaware of it all, which didn't surprise Detective Cardwell one little bit. Without a word she was taken into the lounge where she sat miserably on a sofa, clutching a hankie. Detective Cardwell thought that Emily was right when she described Daisy without her make-up as having the look of a rat.

'What do you want?' she said to the detective, sobbing. 'I've lost my babies, I've lost my husband, my make-up, my clothes . . . what else is there left to lose?'

Detective Cardwell could have named a few other things but instead he ordered tea and toast with butter and marmalade.

'I don't eat carbohydrates,' said Daisy. 'I don't want to lose my figure as well.'

Nevertheless, when the tea and buttered toast and marmalade turned up she ate the whole lot without complaint and colour returned to her cheeks.

'Better?' asked Detective Cardwell.

'Yes.' She let out another sob.

'Good. Now, I would like you to tell me about the visit you had from Doris Harper.'

'This isn't about Ronald, then?' asked Daisy.

'No, I'm conducting a missing persons inquiry and we believe your daughters are among the victims.'

'Oh, my days,' said Daisy, sitting bolt upright and brightening a little. 'Then you don't think I'm nuts when I tell you that my girls have been changed into zombies?'

'No, I don't think you're nuts,' said Detective Cardwell. 'More toast?'

'Oh, yes please,' said Daisy. 'Nothing has tasted this good in ages.'

'Now,' said Detective Cardwell, after Daisy had tucked into another plate of hot buttered toast, 'would you tell me when you first became aware of the change in your triplets?'

'I know the date, the time and the place,' said Daisy. 'It's stuck forever in my mind. You see, I thought that this Doris Harper was from the make-up department. My cutiekins had been the three peas in a TV commercial, and their skin was stained green, and it wouldn't come off. Anyway, Doris Harper turned up, she made their skin white again all right, blooming zombie white, and—'

'Your daughters told me she had a lamp with her,' interrupted the detective.

'You what?' said Daisy.

'A lamp. A bit like an Aladdin's lamp.'

'Oh, my days, yes, she did. There was a little battle – each of my cutiekins wanted to hold it. You know how children can be – and three as well. There was a little how-do-you-do.'

'Then what?'

'Nothing,' said Daisy. 'Or at least I thought nothing. Like good girls they gave the lamp back. Later I realised something was wrong.'

'I believe she sucked the spirits of your daughters into the lamp. If you could help me get the lamp there is a good chance you will have your girls back to their old selves.'

'Tell me what I need to do and I will do it,' said Daisy.

Detective Cardwell explained the plan. Wisely he left out the bit about Harpella's habit of turning human beings into colourful bunnies when she wasn't changing them into zombies. When he had finished, Daisy

Dashwood stood up, looking like a furious rat.

'I will kill that Doris Harper, that's what I'll do, when I lay my hands on the old witch,' she said.

'That won't be necessary,' Detective Cardwell said. 'You just have to distract her long enough for Emily Vole to get the lamp.'

'Come again?' said Daisy, leaning towards him. 'Did you say Emily Vole?'

Detective Cardwell nodded.

'I knew that little minx was involved in this,' said Daisy. 'Telling lies about Ronald and me, sneaking, squeaking behind our backs. It's because of Emily that my Ronald's been arrested, isn't it?'

'No, Mrs Dashwood,' said Detective Cardwell. 'Emily had nothing to do with the warrant for your husband's arrest. The Fraud Squad has been investigating him for a long time. He is suspected of laundering money through phony companies. The only one that was a proper business was yours.'

'Laundry? I do beauty treatments, not laundry,' said Daisy Dashwood. Then the penny dropped. 'How much trouble is he in?' she asked.

'Up to his neck in it,' said Detective Cardwell.

'He'd better hope you find him before I do,' Daisy snarled.

Chapter Twenty-Two

Emily Vole and Daisy Dashwood stood in front of the old shop. Emily knew a lot about it from the stories Miss String had told her and now, after being briefed by Detective Cardwell, she was as well prepared to deal with a witch as a girl could be. Or so she thought.

Emily knew the keys protected her from bunnification. Her heart thumping, she brought them out of her pocket and quickly went in, followed by Daisy. The shop was dark and dusty, full of cobwebs. It looked as if no one had been there for a hundred years, which was most probably correct. The walls were lined with tiny drawers. Another room, joined to the first, was so dimly lit that it was impossible to see inside.

'Oh, my days,' said Daisy Dashwood. 'This heap of rubbish is what the old bat left you? You're welcome to it.' At that moment the keys leapt from Emily's hand and landed on the floor.

'Ugh!' said Daisy. 'I hate spiders, I really hate them. This place gives me goose bumps.'

It wasn't spiders running about but the keys. Emily watched, dismayed, as they hopped, skipped and scuttled merrily across the wooden floor. She tried to catch them but it was useless. Each one disappeared into the murky gloom. Quite what she was supposed to do without the keys, she hadn't a clue. It may be best to leave, she thought. Too late. Daisy was already in the second room and had pulled aside a curtain to reveal a flight of crooked steps.

'No,' whispered Emily. 'Come back. I've lost the keys.'

Daisy Dashwood wasn't going to be ordered about by Emily Vole, no matter what the detective had told her. Determinedly, she started up the twisted stairs.

Emily followed Daisy. She couldn't very well leave her. Too many people needed to be saved.

Together they climbed the winding staircase. Daisy grumbled about having to wear a bright orange boiler suit. But it was either that or her dressing-gown.

'What would my clients at Paradise Beauty Salon say if they could see me? I mean, *orange*. Oh, my days. It clashes with my skin tone.'

They stopped at the first landing. From the other side of a black-painted door they heard a voice. There was no mistaking to whom it belonged.

'Let me out of here, you tricksy timbers, you double-crossing doors.'

'You witch! I want my little cutiekins back.' Daisy bashed fearlessly at the door.

'Oh no!' said Emily.

'No?' said Daisy. 'I say YES, with bells on, that's what I say. I haven't had a good fight since I was six.'

Suddenly the door gave way. Daisy and Emily went flying in. There stood Harpella, crackling with rage, lightning flashing from her long, flaming hair. Before her she held the spirit lamp. Emily was sure that at any moment Daisy would be bunnified.

Daisy Dashwood charged. She and Harpella wrestled in a blur of clashing colours.

'Don't touch me,' thundered Harpella, as she backed away from the fury of Daisy's attack. 'No one touches me!'

'And no one takes away my three little girls,' screamed Daisy. She grabbed hold of Harpella's flaming locks and pulled them with all her strength while bashing and kicking the old witch. 'I want my three cutiekins back,' she screeched, ignoring Harpella's threats. 'Do you hear me, you old bat of a witch?'

'Get off me,' squealed Harpella. 'Your very touch burns my skin.' She lifted the spirit lamp, ready to bring it down on Daisy Dashwood's head.

Emily had a feeling of everything happening in slow motion and at the same time with great speed.

She rushed forward and jumped as high as she could. She snatched the lamp from Harpella's hand, grabbed hold of Daisy and they ran for the door through which they'd come. To Emily's surprise, it had begun to shrink, becoming smaller and smaller.

By a cat's whisker they escaped before the door disappeared altogether, leaving Harpella trapped on the other side.

They sped down the stairs and, completely out of breath, came to a sudden stop.

'Oh, my days,' said Daisy Dashwood. 'Where are we?'

They were not in the shop, that was for sure. They were in a wood-panelled room. There was a fireplace with a mirror over it and not much else, not even a door.

'Oh, buddleia,' said Emily.

At that moment Daisy caught a glimpse of her reflection in the mirror. Surely that couldn't be herself staring back, could it? A woman with floppy, orange, rabbit's ears? And if that wasn't bad enough, with a small, brown, twitchy nose? And whiskers?

The shriek that Daisy Dashwood let out shattered the glass in the mirror and, on that note, she fainted away.

Chapter Twenty-Three

'Buddleia and buddleia again,' said Emily. 'How can you have a room without a door? It's just plain silly.'

At the sound of Emily's voice a huge iron ring in the centre of the floor sprang up and started to throw itself from side to side. Emily clung tightly to the spirit lamp and went to take a closer look. It was a handle to a trap door.

Gloomily it spoke in a deep, rusted voice: 'Pull me,' it said. 'Pull me.'

Emily was trying to do this with one hand while firmly gripping the lamp in the other, when the trap door flew open so suddenly that she and the lamp were sent flying across the room. Emily stood up, dazed. The lamp . . . where was it? It was bumping speedily across the floor towards the trap door.

'Are you all right, my little ducks?'

To Emily's great relief, Fidget's head poked through the trap door. He pounced on the lamp and gave it back to Emily, then threw Daisy Dashwood over his shoulder and clambered back through the trap door to the shop below.

After Daisy had been stretchered out, sneezing, to an ambulance, the shop door jangled shut and all was peaceful with the sound of a century's silence. In the dusk Emily caught a glimpse of something golden flickering. If she wasn't mistaken, it was one of the keys and it had sprouted the smallest pair of dragonfly wings.

Detective Cardwell and Fidget stood still. Even Emily, with all the questions on the tip of her tongue, daren't let one of them slip out. Something extraordinary was about to happen. The key fluttered and hovered between two of the cabinets of tiny drawers. It settled on one, then burrowed into the lock. There was a click as the drawer glided open. Sitting on a dark velvet lining was the most beautiful pair of fairy wings. Emily stared at them until, in a flutter of her eyelid, they had vanished and Detective Cardwell lit up the dark shop in a sparkle of lights, the wings poking out from his coat, his face aglow.

He flew into the air, spinning with delight, hovering above the counter. He returned to the ground and, with a beam of a smile that made him look years younger, lifted Emily off her feet. They rose and sat, laughing, on the top of the cabinets until they heard a thunderous roar from above.

'You tricksy timbers, you double-crossing doors!'

Harpella. Emily couldn't believe she had almost forgotten about her.

'Time to make a move,' said Detective Cardwell. 'The building has a mind of its own and it might decide to release her.'

'Wait – the other keys,' said Emily. She could see them running towards her.

Detective Cardwell's car was parked outside. They piled in and, blue light flashing, sped away.

Emily sat in the back, holding tight to the lamp. It was the most awkward of things. It wriggled about and

farted puffs of bad-smelling smoke.

They were on the motorway when Emily glanced back. There were sparks in the sky. Harpella on her broomstick was bearing down on them. Detective Cardwell put his foot flat on the accelerator, but Harpella was faster. A rip-roaring bolt of lightning hit the side of the car and half the bodywork fell away.

The witch was on top of them. She fired her broomstick again and this time took the roof off the car.

Emily wrestled with the lamp, which was fighting to get free. Her finger found a trigger in the handle and in that instant an idea came to her. Kneeling on the seat of the now open-top car she held the lamp out, hoping Harpella would come even closer.

Certain she could grab the lamp, Harpella took the bait.

'Take this, you evil old witch,' Emily shouted. 'This is for what you did to Miss String!'

And she pulled the trigger.

There was a burst of light and, to Emily's relief, Harpella was lost in a puff of purple smoke.

James Cardwell's car was found upside down, halfway up a bank on the side of the motorway. A report reached Scotland Yard that the car was empty, Detective Cardwell was missing and so were Mr Fidget and Emily Vole. All that was found at the scene of the accident was a large, purple rabbit with pink ears.

'Don't touch me,' it repeated, over and over again.

Chapter Twenty-Four

Detective Cardwell, Emily and Fidget landed safely in a country lane about five miles away. Their escape was thanks to the detective's rediscovered fairy talents.

'We were nearly skinned cod back there,' said Fidget.

Emily, somewhat dazed, was pleased to find she still had hold of the spirit lamp. It rattled as if there was a pebble inside.

Detective Cardwell quickly moved away from her.

'I definitely don't like the sound of that,' he said.

Emily looked inside the lamp and pulled out a huge yellow tooth.

'Swipe me with a kipper,' said Fidget. 'That's the largest dragon's tooth I have ever seen.'

'And one of the most powerful,' added Detective

Cardwell, moving even farther away.

A sound came from the spirit lamp. A sigh. From its bottom, two legs unfolded. On its feet were curly-toed Moroccan slippers. Then two arms sprouted from its sides.

'That dragon's tooth,' said a voice from the lamp, 'has been stuck in the old belly for too long. It's been causing me gyp, I can tell you.'

Emily was so surprised that she dropped the lamp on the ground.

It shook itself.

'Nobody move,' said Detective Cardwell. 'Stay put while I think what to do.'

'It was the tooth, I tell you, the tooth who murdered the fairies, not me,' said the lamp. 'I am an innocent, peace-loving, ill-used, unloved . . .'

'. . . rotten to the core, piece of useless junk,' Fidget muttered. 'If it wasn't for the fishes, I would throw you to the bottom of the ocean and let the barnacles do their worst.'

'I heard that,' replied the lamp. 'I would like it noted, Detective, that *I* was always fond of fairies. That it was

172

Harpella who put that THING,' he pointed at the tooth Emily was holding, 'inside me. It took away all my magical powers.' The lamp lifted its lid and shook itself to make sure there was nothing of the tooth left inside. 'And there was I thinking you might be understanding,' it added sadly, 'knowing what a horrid time I have had of it.'

'Understanding?' said Fidget. 'Horrid time? Blow my whiskers!'

'Fidget,' said Emily. 'You're not helping.'

The lamp rudely stuck its spout out at him.

'Keep your fur on,' said James Cardwell, holding Fidget back. 'We have enough to worry about without a cat fight. For starters, what do we do with that tooth?'

'The bottom of the ocean?' suggested the lamp as it wandered off.

'It must have been a huge dragon,' said Emily, examining the tooth.

At first she didn't notice the wind, but it grew stronger and seemed to be coming from the top of the dragon's tooth. Then the tooth dissolved into a cloud of tiny grey flies and rose into the sky, swerving right and

left as if searching for someone or something. Suddenly, the cloud zoomed off in the direction of the motorway. Five miles away, a large purple and pink rabbit sat up on her haunches and twitched her nose.

The lamp returned to Emily with a small bunch of dandelions.

'These,' said the spirit lamp, 'are for you, my new mistress.'

'New mistress?' said Emily.

'Why, of course. You have saved me from Harpella. She treated me abominably – abominably, I tell you! Look at this dent – here – and here. I received these injuries when she threw me across the room. I am delighted with this outcome. But I must just tell you, I have no genie and I don't do wishes.'

'Oh, fish paste,' said Fidget. 'That's all we need. Another piece of clever-clogs ironmongery.'

They arrived at the Hendon laboratory around lunchtime. Detective Cardwell organised a special train to take the rabbits back to Liverpool Street Station, the hope being that the lamp would transform them to their old selves. James Cardwell was keeping well away from it. Fidget was to go along with Emily to make sure that the lamp didn't get up to any dirty tricks.

'It may be chatty charm itself now,' he said, 'but remember, that lamp has been with Harpella for centuries. The question is, can a lamp change its puff?'

Emily and Fidget were the last to board the train before the whistle went. It was a strange sight indeed to see so many bunnies sitting in cages, each one on a passenger seat. Emily had been given a mobile phone and felt very important. Even the old lady detective with the knitting didn't have a mobile phone. If the lamp wouldn't work then Emily was to text Detective Cardwell: OPERATION BUNNY FAILED. Otherwise, he would be waiting at Liverpool Street Station to take Emily and Fidget back to Podgy Bottom and the Red Lion Hotel.

Clickety-clack went the train, clickety-clack.

Emily gingerly opened the first of the cages. A tubby pink rabbit hopped out.

'I'm on the train, dear,' it said. 'I can't speak now.'

Emily picked up the lamp and pointed it at the rabbit. To her surprise the lamp turned up its spout in disgust.

'That's all we blooming need,' said Fidget. 'I told you it was tricksy.'

'What do you think I am? I am my own lamp, I demand respect.'

'Oh, buddleia,' said Emily, putting the lamp down.

'It would be a good thing if you kept quiet and did your job,' said Fidget.

'It's not my fault that all these people were turned into pink rabbits. Everyone always blames me.'

The lamp was now sitting very close to Emily, its legs sticking out. Fidget looked as though he wanted to throw the thing off the train.

'If you asked nicely,' it continued, 'and rubbed me up the right way . . .'

'Please,' said Fidget, feeling the claws in his paws spring.

'I think,' said Emily, stroking the ears of the tubby bunny, 'I'd better text Detective Cardwell. This is hopeless.'

'Oh-no-it's-not!' said the lamp, and blew a puff of pink smoke.

Suddenly Emily heard snoring. The bunny had turned into a round-tummied gentleman. He was fast asleep and clutching his cage as if it were a briefcase.

'See?' said the spirit lamp to Fidget. 'You only had to ask nicely. It's that little magic word.'

By the time the train arrived at Liverpool Street Station the two carriages were full of sleeping passengers.

'We can't leave them like this,' said Emily. 'If they don't wake up then all our hard work is for nothing.'

'Now,' said the lamp calmly, 'is the time I do my special trick.'

It clicked its fingers together, it stamped its Moroccan slippers on the floor of the carriage and, whizz-bang, everyone woke up, all confused, many still chewing carrots.

Chapter Twenty-Five

F idget had never realised how much his tail meant to him until it was replaced by a pink bunny tail. His balance had gone, he was all wobbly and he didn't feel like himself. When his tail was finally returned, he shook the spirit lamp by the hand.

'I thank you,' he said.

'No, no, no,' said the spirit lamp. 'I thank *you*, for without my dear mistress I would still be a slave – a slave, I tell you.'

Buster Ignatius Spicer was the last of the bunnies to be restored to his old self. He was rather grouchy to discover he again owed his freedom to Emily Vole. It seemed extraordinary to him that Emily, who possessed no magical powers whatsoever, had been courageous enough to steal the spirit lamp from Harpella *and* remove the dragon's tooth inside. And he was grudgingly impressed that she was the new mistress of the lamp.

Buster was now the right size for an eleven-year-old. He looked around the old shop.

'It could do with a clean, Emily,' he said.

'Here,' said Fidget, putting on his apron and handing Buster a broom.

'Me?' said Buster. 'You expect me to do the sweeping?'

'Yes,' said Emily. 'What's wrong with that?'

By the time the three of them had finished, the shop sparkled and gleamed. This, thought Emily, is a new beginning. I will become a detective and, with a bit of practice, I might be able to discover what has happened to my real parents.

The lamp, who loved nothing better than arranging flowers, had put bunches of them on the counter, while Fidget had polished all the cabinets.

'Right,' said Buster. 'Now can I have my wings back?'

Emily took the keys from her pocket, put them on the counter and waited for something to happen. One of the keys took flight and unlocked a cabinet drawer. It glided open.

'Yes!' shouted Buster. 'These will be my wings, you'll see.'

Nothing happened.

'If they were your wings, wouldn't they have fixed themselves to you by now?' said Emily.

The question was no sooner asked than the answer was blown into the shop. Alfred Twizell's wings had found their long-lost owner.

Detective Cardwell hardly recognised the shop when he arrived later that day. Fidget was on a ladder outside carefully repainting the sign above the door. It read: Wings & Co.

'Blow me down,' said Detective Cardwell when he stepped inside. The counter shone, the windows sparkled, but Buster was in a black mood.

'I haven't got my wings back,' he said furiously.

'Perhaps you have to prove yourself, Buster,' said

James Cardwell.

'Me? Buster Ignatius Spicer? Prove myself?'

'The day after tomorrow,' said Emily proudly, 'we will be open for business.'

'Back in the detective business,' said Detective Cardwell, 'after all these years.'

'There is just one thing I have to do first,' Emily said, smiling.

The Dashwoods' house had a For Sale sign attached to the garden gate post.

Daisy Dashwood was recovering from the three operations she had undergone, one to remove the rabbit ears, another to reshape her nose, and finally – the most embarrassing of all – the removal of her bunny tail. She was wrapped in bandages.

When the bell rang, the zombies went to open the door. There stood Emily Vole and Alfred Twizell.

In one voice they said, 'Our mother is a mummy, our daddy is in Spain sorting out his dirty washing. Are you back to look after us, Emily Vole? We still have your ironing board.'

'No,' said Emily firmly.

Daisy Dashwood was lying on the sofa. She looked somewhat smaller than Emily remembered.

'What are you doing here?' she said to Emily. 'This is all your fault . . . after everything we did for you. I have to sell the house, Ronald will probably go to prison and my daughters are still zombies.'

Emily sat down next to her and held up the lamp.

Daisy struggled to sit up.

'I will release the spirits of your three "cutiekins" if you sign some papers,' said Emily.

'You what?' said Daisy.

'It's simple,' said Alfred Twizell. 'It's a document which says that you have no legal rights over Emily Vole.'

Daisy Dashwood signed willingly. A few seconds later, in a whirlwind of noise, Peach, Petal and Plum, her beloved girls, were back to their old selves.

'Nothing else matters,' said Daisy, hugging her three cutiekins, a tear rolling down her cheek.

She saw Alfred Twizell and Emily Vole to the front door and even managed a 'Ta very much'.

As she watched them walk away, she could have sworn that she saw, sticking out of the back of Alfred Twizell's coat, a pair of wings. But that was just plain silly. After all, Daisy Dashwood didn't believe in fairies or daft stuff like that.

Do you?

FIN

Look out for the
Wings & Co
fairy detectives' next case

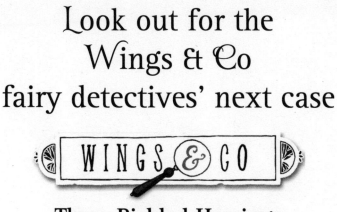

Three Pickled Herrings

What do an orphan, a talking cat and a grumpy fairy
detective have in common? Together they're Wings & Co,
the famous fairy detective agency in Podgy Bottom.

When Sir Walter Cross turns into a human rocket,
the detectives suspect something very fishy is going on.
Soon there's all sorts of hocus pocus and fairy meddling
and Emily, Fidget and Buster find themselves with
not one, but three pickled herrings to solve.

978 1 4440 0373 4

£5.99

www.orionbooks.co.uk